THE VAMPIRE DEBT

USA TODAY BESTSELLING AUTHOR

ALI WINTERS

THE VAMPIRE DEBT

THE VAMPIRE DEBT: BOOK ONE

Published by Rising Flame Press
Edited by Schwartz Fiction Edits and Magnolia Author Services
Cover design & Formatting by Red Umbrella Graphic Designs

This is a work of fiction. Names, characters, businesses, places, events and incidents are the products of the author's imagination or used in a fictitious manner. Any resemblance to actual persons, living or dead, or actual events is purely coincidental.

ISBN-13: 978-1-945238-10-9

www.aliwinters.com

More by Ali Winters

The Hunted series

The Reapers

The Exodus

The Moirai

The Fallen

Flirting with Death

In The End duology

Sound of Silence

Light in Darkness

Shadow World

The Vampire Debt

The Vampire Curse

The Vampire Court

The Vampire Oath

The Vampire Crown

The Vampire Betrayal

Stand Alone

Cast In Moonlight

Favor of the Gods

A Sky of Shattered Stars

Army of the Winter Court

Praise for The Vampire Debt

"A dark and dangerous twist from a timeless classic that will keep you flipping pages and leave you wanting more!"
—CAMEO RENAE, USA Today Bestselling Author

"A dark retelling with a provocative twist that lures you into its pages."
—NATALIA JASTER, author of the Selfish Myths series

"I am completely, utterly, and absolutely obsessed!"
—LEXXY VORPAHL, paranormal romance author

"This book is amazing… I was seriously BLOWN AWAY."
—MICHELLE G., goodreads reviewer

"Conflict, twists and turns and a story that makes you root for the characters yet relate to their flaws at the same time."
—TRISH BENINATO, fantasy author

"[The Vampire Debt] is my ****ing favorite. Everything about this book is brilliant."
— KITTY GALLANT, romance author

"Ms. Winters took my breath away!!! This is going to steal away your heart and mind as well!! These characters are delicious and will tug upon your heartstrings!"
— MICHELLE F., goodreads reviewer

"Sink your teeth into this blood-pumping story of love, loss, and redemption. You won't be disappointed."
— JESIKAH SUNDIN, award winning author

Shadow World

Nightwich
CASTLE

S U N T

Progsdale

Durford

Littlemire

Valeburn

MOUNTAINS

Sangate

Gloamfarrow

Windbury

Galeport

Crescent Isle

Murhelm

Stormvale

N

For Jesikah

CHAPTER ONE

CLARA

It isn't the sound of the front door slamming that wakes me. Or even the sound of Father as he drunkenly stomps through the house toward his room to finally collapse, face down, onto his bed just before dawn. I grew accustomed to those noises long ago. Instead, it's the sharp pain of hunger that pulls me from a deep sleep.

I lift my book from my chest and close it. The leather is worn smooth from use over the years. It's the only one I have left from before life went to hell. I brush my hand over the cover, wrap it up in an old cloth, and place it under my pillow.

I fell asleep reading again. Father would have my head if he knew I used one of our few remaining candles.

Sliding my legs over the edge of the bed, I tiptoe across the floor, the wooden slats cold beneath my feet. I move silently to avoid waking Kathrine. She stretches out as soon as I'm gone, pulling the blankets closer toward her, and lets out a soft sigh. I pause, not moving, barely even daring to breathe as I wait to make sure she's still fast asleep.

Kathrine stirs and rolls to her side.

"Clara?" she mumbles, still mostly asleep.

"It's early, go back to sleep," I shush her gently. When she doesn't make a noise or movement of protest, I quickly slip into my worn, deerskin trousers and shrug into a thick shirt, not bothering to tie the laces at the hollow of my throat.

I pick up my boots from behind the door and slip out of the room, closing it slowly behind me while trying to keep the old hinges from screeching.

I turn to face the small room that serves as our main living area, kitchen, and dining room in one. A far cry from the luxury we used to have. The room reeks of spilled spirits. Several dirty cups and a mess of gambling tokens lay scattered across our table. I wonder how much of our meager stash of money Father gambled away last night.

I shake away the thoughts and my blooming anger—it doesn't matter. It never matters. There's nothing I can do to change it.

Plopping down on the bench beside the fireplace and the dying embers that barely give off any heat, I tug my boots on. They conform to the shape of my legs perfectly, even if the leather is worn around the seams. If I can make them last through the coming summer, then I should be able to stash away enough coin to buy a used pair and not have Father or Kathrine notice.

My guilt over such things has long since vanished, especially since it had somehow fallen on my shoulders to supply all our food and needs and bring home enough money for Father to lose in his near-nightly games.

I don't even try to be quiet now as I stand, flinging my cloak over my shoulders. I head for the door, pausing to snatch up a small piece of stale bread left out on the counter. I pull my knife from my pocket and slice off the slightly molded bit then shove it into my mouth as I open the door with one hand. I snatch up my arrows and close the door behind me.

It's chilly in the watery light of morning, but it is enough to keep the demons that haunt the forest at bay—but just barely. While it's still early in autumn, the mornings have already begun to cool.

I walk along the dirt road, avoiding the muddy patches as much as possible. It is mostly deserted this time of day, with only an occasional cart or rider. Nevertheless, I skirt around the town to avoid being seen and turn into the grassy field that separates our small village of Littlemire from the Shade forest.

I crouch low, hurrying through the field, trying to keep from being noticed. Going into the forest is forbidden. That territory doesn't belong to us. Though the butcher and the clothier know I

3

go there almost daily, they keep that to themselves because I bring them meat and fur far cheaper than anyone else.

Father doesn't care what I spend my days doing, so long as I keep bringing home money and food. I think Kitty would like to think I have some sort of honorable job in town that provides for us.

Once I hit the trees, I stand to full height and jog until I'm certain no one can see me. I pull an arrow from my quiver and knock it into my bow as I walk with near-silent steps, eyes scanning for birds or rabbits, or some other woodland creature that might make a decent meal, as well as the wild beasts, said to roam the forests hunting anyone who dares stray too far into the woods.

But those are old wives' tales, stories told to children to keep them from wandering too far from home. They are no more real than the stories about princes rescuing girls who have suffered lives no one should have to endure. No more real than tales of unicorns and fairy godmothers, poor servant girls who are found out to be long lost princesses, or even colorful worlds, where the grasses are bright green instead of a dried yellowish hue, of flowers that blanket the countryside, or skies so blue they are the color of gems.

In those tales, the monsters are always defeated.

No, those things aren't real. What is real is a perpetually gray sky that always has the feeling of being on the brink of a downpour. What is real is a world that was not only born of demons and monsters, but is ruled by them.

4

A mile in, and I've seen nothing so far. I roll my shoulders, then my neck, letting the tension in my muscles ease a bit. A little further, and I set a few small traps, then climb a tree and wait for something to cross my path. I'm not good with an arrow by any means, but sometimes I get lucky.

I'm already tired, and my stomach still aches. Thankfully, the small scrap of bread I ate is enough to keep it from grumbling and scaring off the prey.

Slinging my bow over my shoulder, I shove my gloves into my pockets and climb a tree with thick, sturdy branches.

My fingers are already stiff from the chill, but morning dew sticks to the bark, making it soft and impossible to climb with gloves. At any rate, I'll need the accuracy of unburdened fingers once I reach my perch.

It takes me only a few minutes to find a branch sturdy enough to support my weight, yet high enough to avoid easy detection.

I settle in, ready my bow, and knock an arrow.

Hours pass, and weariness sets in. I debate on giving up and going into town to see if I can find a little something no one will miss, when a rustle of leaves brings me to attention.

A fat, white rabbit pops its head out from beneath the brush.

In a painfully slow movement, to avoid creating even the slightest creak from my bow, I pull my arrow back, ready to let it fly, and stop when the distant sound of someone humming a lullaby reaches me. Easing the pull I have on the arrow, I glance around, doing my best to avoid moving too much.

My eyelids grow heavy, and I find myself wanting to drift off. I jolt, sucking in a breath, and hold it.

Damn it. That was too close. My heart pounds and it's all I can do to remain calm.

I look back to where I saw the rabbit to find a young woman sitting there. She's humming. Her shoulders move with ever so slight movements as if she's weaving a crown of flowers or some other harmless thing.

But she is no innocent.

She is a nightmare come to life. She is everything that is wrong with this world.

I watch her for a long moment, unsure what my next move will be. If I jump down and run, she will spot me. But my leg is beginning to cramp, and if I don't leave soon, I'm sure my stomach will start to growl.

There's only one thing I can do. A cold sweat breaks out across my forehead at the thought of following through.

Slowly, I lift my bow. The fletching of my arrow grazes my cheek as I pull it back. The bowstring groans, halting my movements and my breath. I wait several heartbeats making sure the monster in my sights doesn't notice my presence before it's too late.

My original purpose for coming into the woods today has already been forgotten.

Long, golden hair flows down her back in waves, almost as pale as her skin. A stark contrast to her dark red dress — so dark it's almost black, like a thick pool of fresh blood.

How fitting.

To most eyes, she would appear to be nothing more than a young woman.

But I know better. Her impossibly graceful movements and her perfect stillness give her away for what she is.

She is a wolf in sheep's clothing, only something far more dangerous and deadly — beautiful on the outside, but grotesque and twisted inside. From where I sit perched in my tree, she could be reading as she sits in the grass. Though I know better. She is sucking the life out of some poor, defenseless animal, watching the life leave its eyes as it can do nothing but gaze back at her in terror.

She continues to hum as she feeds, a tune so familiar and haunting. It makes my head pound. It steals whatever hesitation I might still possess.

I pull my arrow back a fraction more, my muscles straining. Then I let go.

The second I do, she stills and starts to turn her head toward me. *Demons of the Otherworld help me* — if she moves before it reaches her — I am dead.

The arrow sails through the air, and I hold my breath. It hits the mark, just to the left of her spine, piercing her heart. She hovers for a moment before falling face-first into the ground with a soft thud.

Her hair fans out around her in a gold nimbus.

I brush the back of my hand across my forehead, wiping away the sweat that beaded.

I've got to go before others come for her. Before anyone finds out what I've done and finds me here.

I leap down from the tree and sling my bow around my shoulders. I turn to run, but some morbid curiosity holds me back. I need to make sure she's truly dead and not faking it. Years of waiting to seek revenge on my mother's killer, and it's over with the flick of my wrist. It's almost too easy to believe.

Of course, there's no way to know for sure that she is the vampire responsible... but aren't they all? They are all equally as terrible... all guilty of the same crimes.

I make my way toward it, as slow as I can manage, trying not to make any noise. I reach her and look down. Her flaxen hair is splayed all around her. Red slowly leeches its way in and through the strands, darkening them as it spreads.

With the toe of my boot, I tap her side, ready to bolt. I scrutinize the arrow sticking out from her back. If I leave it here, then it can be traced back to me. I have to take it even though I can't use it again—the blood from this abomination would taint any game I used it on.

I roll her over. Her face, partially obscured by hair, is serene. She looks like she's sleeping, but her lips are stained red with blood. The dead rabbit in her hand stares, unseeing. Her fingers are all but crushing it. The sight makes me want to retch.

I reach for the arrow, grabbing it low on the shaft and wrench it from the monstrosity. It makes a sickening slurping sound as it comes free. I shove it into my quiver.

Some of the beast's blood is on my hands. I crouch and wipe it off the best I can on the frozen blades of grass.

Then I turn and run. I run and don't stop until I reach the edge of town.

My breath comes heavy and I earn a few strange looks from the townsfolk, but I keep moving, wending my way through them, determined to lose myself in the crowd.

My hands shake, but I'm smiling, is probably too wide, but I can't help it. The mixture of nerves, of fear, of vindication, is strong. For two years, I've been going out into those woods every chance I got to hunt. There was always a small hope I would come across one of the monsters... waiting for the one who killed Mother to return, so I could repay that life debt.

I refuse to be a food source for them. I refuse to be shoved down to the bottom of the food chain because evolution dealt vampires a winning hand long ago. I refuse to allow them to be the only ones able to seek out justice for crimes.

I make it to an alley where there are always boxes, and garbage piled up, and toss in my bow and arrows into the rubbish. I hesitate, but only for a second. It's a waste of money, but I can't risk having them traced back to me. It would spell death, not only for me but for my family as well. I quickly remove my jacket and the outer layer of clothes to mask my scent alongside the bow.

My own clothes are wrinkled and smell of sweat. I smooth them down as best I can, then head back out into the throng of people milling about in the square. This time, making sure I am seen by as many people who know me as possible. I even go so far as to greet some I don't know.

I am tired and hungry and am in desperate need of a bath, but it is still many hours before I can make my way home.

Though I move slowly from vendor to vendor, my heart still pounds wildly from what I did.

Today, I have made my own justice.

Today, I have done what others in this town have only ever talked about but are never brave enough to do.

Today, I have signed my own death warrant.

I've just killed a vampire.

CHAPTER
TWO
CLARA

Vampires rule our world, and demons haunt the shadows. The vampires come and go as they please, and we humans are little more than chattel. Our purpose is to serve them and to feed them. For the most part, we remain safe as long as we follow their laws they set forth, and keep our heads down, and remember our place.

We humans travel between villages on rare occasions, because getting caught outside after nightfall has deadly consequences. In the dark, we are playthings for whatever demons we are unlucky enough to cross paths with.

Once a year, during the claiming, the vampire court will come to our rundown village and demand a human, or several. Some even gladly go, willing to be servants to the monsters.

The thought of it sends a shiver crawling down my spine. No one knows what becomes of any of the claimed. Perhaps they do live in a world of luxury doting on their vampires, enjoying soft, comfortable plush beds at night. Or maybe they are nothing more than a snack for the long ride home, or worse. I can always imagine worse, but for now, I shove the thoughts aside.

A drop of water splatters on my cheek. It is the first sign of rain—*real* rain—after this endless bog of mist plaguing us all week. I think at this point, I'd rather be soaked through then perpetually damp.

Most shop owners are at the entrance, attempting to lure any and all passersby inside. The more desperate of them have spilled out onto the sidewalk, with makeshift booths.

Passing several, I lift a scarf from a woman too busy to notice me as she deals with a particularly unpleasant vendor. Then a cloak carelessly set aside by another. I turn the corner wrapping the cloak and scarf around me before anyone can notice the items are missing.

I shuffle through the crowd of villagers keeping my head down. I glance around, unable to shake the feeling that a shadow hovers just outside my peripheral. My shoulder bumps a man. He grunts rudely, muttering under his breath.

Giving him a simpering smile, I mutter my apologies to him as I place one hand on his arm, distracting him from the fact that my other hand is in his pocket pulling out his pathetically

12

light bag of coins. I hadn't meant to run into him. Usually, remorse presses down on my chest when I steal, though with the particularly nasty ones, the feeling is lessened when snatching up a pocket watch or lifting a bag of coin.

With a bag this light, it seems he spent most of his money trying to make himself look rich, or he's too cheap to part with much when he deigns to visit this part of our little village.

As if any of us care about rich fabrics and ostentatious finery. A few citizens in Littlemire are lucky enough to enjoy a hot meal and a warm bed with enough legroom to stretch out every night. For the rest of us, a roof over our heads, enough coal to keep our homes heated against the worst of the chill, and a hot meal a few nights a week is the best we can hope for.

He starts to turn away, sneering at me, and I take the man's antique watch for good measure.

I would never steal from someone struggling to get by, knowing the pain of going to bed hungry for far too many nights to inflict that kind of hardship on someone else. I've always made it a point to take only from those who can spare a little something without putting them in dire straights.

I glide away from him and lose myself in the crowd. A moment later, the man's outcry cuts through the din of voices. "Someone stole my watch—my coin as well! Where did that thief go?"

Perhaps I was a little heavy-handed today—a little too greedy.

Having run out of our supply of salted meats and pickled vegetables, we are close to starving. It's been all I could do for the last week to avoid Father's temper. Always demanding money and food as if we were still rich.

Though I'm more likely to get caught, it looks as though I'll have to pickpockets for at least the next week, possibly two. I'll have to avoid hunting for game in the woods. I can't let anything connect me to the death of that monster. To get caught would be instant death by the closest vampire... and it will not be a good death.

I duck into the nearest alley and crouch behind some boxes and wait until the furious man gives up looking for me.

I still can't shake the feeling that a shadowy presence is hovering, watching, waiting to pounce. It stalks close behind, breathing down my neck. I spin to look back and catch whoever or whatever it is, but I'm alone.

Shame colors my cheeks. Shame and fear that the vampire has already been found. That I've already been discovered. That they will find me and demand my life in exchange for its cursed life. I scowl—*a human life in exchange for that of a beast.*

It is only hunger that drives me from hiding and into town.

But I've gotten rid of my bow and the arrows that could link me to what I've done. They will be buried deep under a mountain of garbage and rotted food by the end of the day. It's a shame, I'll have to buy more if I ever hope to hunt in the woods

14

again.

Reaching up, I pull back my scarf and let my long, dark hair fall around my shoulders. I turn the scarf around, hiding the drab gray side and showing off the deep red of the other side. It will stand out just enough so that he can look me straight in the eye and still doubt it was me. After all, what thief in their right mind would wear such a color that would draw attention to them?

I take a deep breath and stand ready to move back out into the crowd. I think I have enough of a haul for today. I stick my hand into my pocket and pull out a few coins—just enough for a hot sweet roll or two. It's a little decadent, but this week has been especially sparse. I'll bring one home to Kathrine. She will enjoy the treat.

My mouth already waters at the thought of it—the warm, sweet bread, lightly coated with icing melting on my tongue.

The man continues making a scene a few stalls from where I emerge. I stroll on, taking my time as I pass each vendor until I get to the potter. A hand falls heavy on my shoulder, and I freeze. Not sure if I should fight, run, or play innocent.

Then a warm voice whispers close to my ear. "What has you looking so ruffled today, Clara?"

His fingers flick a lock of hair over my shoulder.

I turn to face Xander, giving him one of my rare but honest smiles. I shrug with one shoulder and let the back of my hand brush against his so that it would look like nothing more than an accidental contact to anyone paying attention. I long to hold his hand, or link arms, instead of hiding our affections to avoid a scandal.

"Just on my way to the baker," I say casually, taking a few steps toward the patisserie. Xander sticks close to my side.

He gently elbows me. "Up to the usual then," he says with a knowing smirk.

We both glance toward the center square, and the man I pickpocketed yelling even louder.

Xander jerks a thumb in the man's direction. "I don't suppose you happen to know what all that fuss is about, would you?"

"Not in the least," I say, sniffing once, feigning offense and continuing on.

Together, we walk in silence past several more shop owners peddling their wares. "You need to be more careful," he whispers.

I choose to ignore his warning. I'll do this as long as I must to make ends meet and keep my family fed and clothed.

As we reach the patisserie, I inhale deeply. My stomach clenches at the sweet smells wafting from inside. "Do you want a sweet roll? It's on me today."

Then before I know what's happening, he spins me into the alley and grabs my hips, pulling me to him. My chest is pressed up against his, and his arms wrap tightly around my waist. My back presses up against the rough, stone wall.

"Do you promise that it's *on you?*" he practically purrs

the words into my ear, sending a shiver down my body. His words make little sense, but the intended meaning shines clear in his tone.

"Why, Mr. Callowell! You are indecent," I say in mock horror.

Up close, his hazel eyes shine, and I can see the smattering of freckles on the bridge of his nose.

I hastily swat at his arm and step to the side, freeing myself from his hold. Heat spreads across my cheeks, and his grin widens, happy he received the reaction he wanted from me.

"Don't do that." I bite the bottom of my lip and look around to see if anyone was watching. "What if someone sees?"

He groans and drops his head back, running a hand through his auburn hair in an unsuccessful attempt to smooth the mussed locks. "I don't care what they think. You are mine, and there's nothing they can do to stop it."

"But what if they tell your parents? They'll never approve."

"They'll have no choice," he murmurs sweetly, and wholly unconcerned. "After allowing each of my brothers to wed whomever they please, they will have to let me have my choice. And I choose you." He looks stern. "You turned twenty-one months ago; you don't have to stay at home anymore." His face darkens at the thought of my situation.

He's right. I could have left years ago.

But not really.

I could never forgive myself if I left Kathrine alone with Father and no one else to look after her.

Xander's family is well off enough that I will never have to worry about Father again. I can escape him and live to a ripe old age with the man I love in peace. With Kathrine in my care, she will never have to worry about an empty belly ever again. And maybe I can finally get her the medicine she needs to be rid of her affliction once and for all.

"Come on," I say, pulling him into the bakery with me. "Let's get those sweet rolls."

We go in and I gladly hand over the coins in exchange for two large pastries. Then the two of us retreat to the side of the building to enjoy our snacks. I savor each bite, forcing myself to go slow. Xander is finished by the time I have eaten half. I take out a handkerchief and wrap the remainder in it, then stuff it in my bag.

"How's Kitty doing?" Xander asks, knowing exactly why I'm saving it.

I toe the ground with my mud-covered boot, kicking a pebble and watching it skitter away. Glancing up out of the corner of my eye, I say, "She's struggling. The damp is making it harder for her to breathe."

He nods. I adore him for asking because I know the subject makes him uncomfortable.

"I'd better get going," I say, pushing away from the mist-slicked brick wall of the building.

I step out into the cobblestone street, but his hand catches mine and pulls me back.

"Meet me tomorrow night at the usual place?" he asks.

It's hardly romantic meeting each other in the old barn behind my house. But it's our spot. The one we've been going to for years. I nod and he presses his lips to mine, kissing me hard. I straighten the lapels of his cutaway morning coat.

Stepping back, I break the moment, moving out of his reach and throwing a wicked smile over my shoulder.

"Be careful," he says, all teasing and playfulness vanishing from his voice.

I raise a brow at his uncharacteristic concern. He always cares, yet this is over the top even for him. "Aren't I always?"

"I'm serious, Clara. Tonight is the first day of the claiming."

The claiming. *Shit*. How could I be so stupid as to have forgotten? My timing killing that abomination couldn't have been worse. I need to get home and fast. The blood drains from my face so quickly that it makes me dizzy. I turn away from Xander, but not before he sees.

"Are you all right?"

I nod, plastering a smile to my face. It's false. It pains me to be less than genuine with him. But he mustn't find out. No one can. It seems to put him at ease because he returns the expression. Then turning, I run out of our hideaway and into the crowd.

19

Slowing to a walk, I near the edge of the town when the unmistakable clatter of a carriage and hooves on the cobblestone road halt me in my tracks.

I swallow the lump of dread back down as a single carriage, led by two dappled grays, heads my way.

It turns from the main road and heads into the square. I stop and push back up into the stone of the nearest building, dropping my chin.

I don't move a muscle... I barely so much as breathe as I wait for it to pass. It's only a brief moment, but it feels like an eternity as the memories of my arrow finding its mark keep flashing through my mind over and over again.

The clatter of hooves stops in the center of the square opposite the fountain. While everyone else inches closer, I turn and run. I don't make it far down the road before another carriage is headed my way, followed by another and three more behind it. They've all come. Every vampire royal, plus whatever others accompany them.

I shudder at the thought of so many untamed monsters in our midst.

In an effort to avoid them, I cross the road and jump the fence running through the Bennet's field. He'd throw a fit if he found out, so it's a good thing that he, like the rest of Littlemire, is currently distracted by vampires.

As I near the weather-worn house, no bigger than a cottage

20

that I call home, I slow to a walk, easing my panting breaths to a slow, natural rhythm. Smoke curls from our tilted chimney, and, for a second, I can almost believe that Mother is inside preparing to start dinner, that Father is in his office working on his books, and Kathrine is curled up in a chair before the fire, reading.

I hear voices inside, Father's and... another I've never heard before. I look around. There is no sign of hoof prints near our home or any leading to the barn.

A feeling of unease settles in my gut as I approach.

CHAPTER
THREE
CLARA

Approaching the door, I hesitate for a long moment. Butterflies flutter in my gut, and my nerves are on high alert. I shake my head, telling myself it's fine.

I push the door open and step in. It takes a moment for my eyes to adjust to the rushlight's dim glow as I remove my cloak and hang it beside the door.

"Ah, Clara," my father's voice chimes as though he's delighted to see me. Except, he's never happy to see me. "There you are."

My hands freeze in mid-motion as suspicion makes my blood run cold. He is up to something.

I quickly bunch my hands into fists and turn to face Father and his guest, forcing my face into a blank mask.

The man at Father's side is tall and quite possibly the most handsome man I've ever laid eyes on. His dark hair is perfectly cut and swept back, it's not long enough to be tied but, almost. On anyone else, it would look unkempt, but it only adds to his sophisticated appearance. His clothes are tailored, and much finer than anything Xander's family owns.

He must be from a neighboring town, most likely the cousin of one of the more well-off families here, no doubt one of their unwitting cousins who don't know better than to stay away from Father. What is a man of his stature doing in our dirty little cottage?

Dread pools over me. That could only mean Father is getting us further into debt. It won't be long until I can no longer keep up with his spending, it's nearly impossible as it is. I don't remember the last time his gambling did anything other than empty our already lacking accounts.

Our guest eyes me up and down, assessing me as if I'm a horse at market. His nostrils flare, and his eyes grow wide for a split second before narrowing. I straighten my back as he casts his judgment upon me.

I can only imagine what he's thinking as he takes me in wearing men's breeches and riding boots. I've obviously come back in from the forest. The mud on my boots gives that away. And without my bow, there's no doubt he thinks I've been out trying to catch rabbits with my teeth.

His upper lip twitches.

Finally releasing me from his impenetrable gaze, he pulls a watch from his vest pocket and looks at the time, then replaces it. "I must be going."

Father's eyes go wide as he speaks in his friendliest tone, but I can still make out the desperation in his words. "Surely, Mr. Devereaux, you will stay a while longer and allow me the chance to regain what I have lost?"

The man stares down his nose at me as he adjusts his gloves, barely paying attention to Father. "I am afraid that will not be possible at this time. I have other business I must attend to."

The longer he watches me with cold detachment and eyes that scrutinize and judge, the more my annoyance turns to anger. Surely after this evening, he knows the kind of man my father is, and he knows that I must be doing the best I can with this life I was born into...

Then I frown. Why on earth would I care what this man thinks? A man of so little honor that he would take the last of our money because of a stupid betting game... a man who could lose ten times as much and not feel its effects.

His nostrils flare and his eyes narrow. The howling of lesser demons starts up in the distance as the sun begins to lower.

"Very well, Mr. Devereaux, do be careful until you are settled for the night," Father says, unaware of the strange exchange between us.

I remain rooted in place as the man sneers at me before turning to my father and giving him a dark smile. "It was a pleasure doing business with you. I will return soon to settle the debt," he says in a rich, languid tone.

"It is a shame you came into town on the same day the vampires did." Father shakes his head, sneering at his glass of wine before taking a large gulp and finishing it off.

Mr. Devereaux raises one dark brow, finally looking away from me to Father and says, "Indeed."

They shake hands then he strides toward the door. His gaze cuts to me, narrowing with menace. His eyes look almost black in the dim lighting, save for the faintest hint of deep blue framed by thick, black, enviable lashes. Then he's out the door and gone before I can begin to understand what his problem with me could possibly be.

"Close the door and get in here, girl. You're letting all the heat out," Father snaps.

I jump into action, closing the door after our guest. Then I look down at my hands smudged with dirt. He must think I'm nothing more than some lowly servant. I'm sure I have dirt on my face as well. I rub a spot on the side of my finger. Not dirt. But dried blood from when I pulled my arrow free from that beast.

"Where have you been? I thought I'd told you not to wander today," he scolds.

My head snaps up. He acts as if we have all the money in the world, yet it's only thanks to my 'wandering' that we still have a roof over our heads and food in our bellies most days. "I was out getting this," I retort, flinging the small bag of coins at him then turn toward the room to check on Kathrine.

"That's it?" he demands from behind.

"Yes, I had to get Kathrine's medicine—" I keep my fists at my side to keep from clutching the small vial of liquid in my pocket, lest he take it from me to sell.

"You don't worry about that. You know to bring home every coin. I am the head of this household, and I will take care of the necessities."

"Then take care of them," I bite out, rounding on him. "Quit gambling our money away. If it weren't for me and what I can manage to bring home, we would have starved a long time ago." There is so much I want to say to him. Though it's the same every time. The same fight, the same words that fall on deaf ears. I am stopped before I can say anything more by a resounding slap across my cheek that sends my head snapping to the side.

"Watch your mouth. If it weren't for me, you'd have died on the streets after your mother was taken."

He says the words as though he's some kind of savior who rescued me from that fate, and like I'm not his daughter.

My teeth cut the inside of my cheek and the coppery taste of blood touches my tongue. There will be a bruise by morning. My face burns from the strike, already swelling. I only pivot and head into the room I share with my sister.

26

Kitty sits up a little straighter in bed when she sees me enter the room. A smile brightens her face until it's stolen by a cough.

"Come, sit," she says, holding out her hands and beckoning me to her side. "Tell me, is that strange man gone?"

I sit next to her and brush her hair back behind her ear. "And what do you know of him?" I ask.

"Well..." She clasps her hands together and leans forward, whispering in a hushed voice even though we are the only ones in the room. "I know he's been here all day. He showed up shortly after you left. He brought a chill in with him, so I had to excuse myself to rest, but from what I've gathered, he is in town for business that must be of a demon's making because he would not speak a word of it to Father."

I smile and pat her leg. "Don't go getting yourself riled up. Mr. Devereaux is gone. I don't think we'll be seeing him again."

The grin I wear strains across my face, and I hope she can't tell. Her superstitions about demons playing a role in people's everyday lives are going to get her worked up until she falls ill again.

Standing, I head to the small armoire we share and rifle through it for fresh clothes to change into—ones not covered in a layer of dust and mud.

"Clara," she scolds gently. "What aren't you telling me? How much did Father lose this time?" Her words are as bitter as I feel.

"I don't know." I slowly turn to face her. "Enough that Mr.

Devereaux will be back in a few days to settle."

Her pale cheeks turn pink, then red. "We will never be married at this rate if Father continues to spend every penny! What dowry does he expect to give?"

I already know the answer. He's not. He thinks it as a waste of money.

Marriage is our only escape from this hell, the only way we can ever be well and truly safe away from Father's wrath and senseless spending. I think about the stash of money I have hidden under the floorboards. It will take a while yet to obtain what I need for us both.

I must plan this just right. First, Xander must obtain his family's blessing, then I can find a suitable match for Kitty. Perhaps we could even have a double wedding. She would love that.

"Do not stress yourself over this. You'll make yourself sick." I cross over to her and cup her cheek. "I will take care of you. Never forget that."

Once we are away from here, Kathrine will finally have a chance at living her life as a true lady, just like she deserves.

CHAPTER
FOUR
ALARIC

My carriage pulls up as I step over the threshold of the dilapidated hovel that man had the gall to act as though it were a palace. A second later, Mr. Valmont's gruff voice rings out. All of the false pleasantries he'd used during my visit are now gone.

"Close the door, girl. You're letting the heat—" he snarls, his words cut off as the door slams shut.

The carriage opens, and Lawrence Harkstead smiles from within, practically lounging on his side. I climb in and close the door, sitting across from my old friend just as the horses take off.

I shudder, glad to be out of that horrid place. "Perfect timing, as usual," I say.

Lawrence scoffs and looks out of the window to the rapidly

vanishing dwelling. He wrinkles his nose, his voice full of disdain as he asks, "What in the depths of the Otherworld were you doing in such a rundown shack? Have you grown so bored with life that you are befriending peasants now?"

He lounges back, his long blond hair slightly mussed, his waistcoat remains straight, his shirt immaculate, though his tailcoat lay crumpled in a heap next to him. He has been feeding, and by the look of that smug grin on his face, feeding well. This visit has reminded me exactly why I don't partake in this ritual.

"I will be leaving tomorrow and taking Rosalie with me back to Windbury," I say, ignoring his goading questions.

"What? *Before* the claiming? You arrive a day early and leave the day it begins. I was under the impression you were finally going to relax and join us in the festivities."

I rest my head against the back and stare unseeing at the black material of the ceiling. "I have no wish to claim any of these humans. Besides, you know how Rosalie feels about it."

That horrid girl's face flashes in my mind's eye. Her entrance had managed to surprise me when so little does anymore. The man had failed to mention he had a second daughter. Not that it would have changed anything. I had no interest in the lot of them.

My anger flares again at remembering the faint scent of vampire blood that lingered somewhere on her person. Had that been of her doing? I scoff inwardly.

She's slight of build and doesn't seem to have anything

30

extraordinary about her that would enable her to pull off such a feat. Chances were the human had brushed up against the real slayer while doing whatever it is that her ilk did with their days.

"Again? Elizabeth will not be pleased. She won't allow this to go on forever. You must claim a human, even if you only claim one and drain them on the way home — it's about reminding them of our power as much as it is about survival."

Lawrence would undoubtedly lecture me until the end of the claiming if I had told him my original plan was to leave tonight. I have no wish to collect a debt from that pathetic man. I have more money than I could spend in several lifetimes. Even then, Elizabeth would not allow me to fall from the status she has set for me. Taking money from a poor man who doesn't know when to stop gambling the funds he should have been spending on his family's well-being holds no interest.

It was only that trace of blood that has me staying.

"It is a truth universally acknowledged, that a single vampire in possession of a good fortune, must be in want of a mortal snack," he says with a dramatic hand gesture, then slumps back, legs sprawled.

"I survive by willing offerings just fine." It's the same thing every year, the same conversation. And I am weary of it all.

"This isn't about your ego. It's about tradition. It's what we are — *who* we are. You can't continue to use Rosalie as a reason to shun our ways."

"They are not my ways."

"Except they are, my dear friend. You are one of us, no matter what you choose to tell yourself."

I say nothing, and the silence drags on between us for a long moment. I refuse to lose the last bits of my humanity. I refuse to be anything other than what Rosalie wants me to be. Her fate, after all, was my doing.

Lawrence sits up folding his arms across his chest and glares at me until I straighten to meet his gaze.

"If your objection is the unwilling few, there are plenty of parties." A grin spreads across his lean face. "They have more than enough willing prey who would give just about anything to have the mark, and so much more. Especially from you."

My lip curls at his intended meaning. I might try my damnedest to hold on to my humanity by only drinking from the willing. The last thing I desire is to let one of those pathetic worshipers drape themselves all over me. All they want is the mark—they do not care whose mark it is.

Lawrence drones on about the endless parties that are to come, oblivious to how much I detest the idea with each passing word.

The horses' hooves clop along on the cobblestone road. I focus on the rhythm of the sound as I turn my attention to the passing scenery, dark stone buildings, slanted roofs, and hardly a human in sight. A typical occurrence before sunset to be sure.

Pathetic. The humans only give lesser demons more strength by offering their fear.

Soon the town gives way to trees lining the road. The cobblestones turn to dirt.

As much as I long to leave this place and return home, I must find the mortal who owes the life debt.

But then that girl... no, she was not a girl but rather a young woman dressed in men's trousers, shirt, and jacket. The clothes were large on her, making her appear smaller and younger than she no doubt is. She smelled of earth and mist and sweet treacle.

With the defiant tilt of her chin, she had actually looked down her nose at me. It was absurd. For a second, I thought she recognized me for the vampire I am, and not the rich son of a banker her Mr. Valmont had assumed I was. But there had been no trembling in her stance, no cowering, and no adoration.

Again, my mind goes back to the scent of vampire blood that lingered on her, faint though as it was. I cannot leave here until I know if they were slain by her hand, as unlikely as it would seem, or another's.

Most importantly, *who* had been murdered in cold blood. I will get the answers I seek tonight, and tomorrow I will find the mortal responsible.

I knock on the roof and the driver pulls the carriage to a stop in the middle of town. The sudden stop has Lawrence speechless, cutting off in mid-sentence.

33

"Thank you for your impeccable timing as always, but I have some other business to attend to." He raises a brow as I climb down out of the carriage. "I will see you after the claiming."

Lawrence lowers a window and sticks his head out, saying, "At least think about claiming one."

One human in this city has blood on their hands, and they will pay one way or another by the court's decree. Though it is not a punishment I intend to inflict. I nod anyway, hoping it will be enough to make him drop the subject. "I will think about it."

Another knock on the side of the carriage and it's moving once more.

I stay standing in the abandoned streets until it is out of sight.

In truth, I do not know where to begin, so I walk along the edges and follow the buildings. The night falls early this time of year, and it brings with it a chill. Wandering around the empty streets for hours makes me eternally grateful I have avoided coming to these towns all these years.

These humans choose to live in squalor, their buildings coated in grime and dirt. Paper and other detritus litter the gutters. For a moment, it has me regretting my decision to stay in this town and search out the guilty party.

And then I catch the tang of blood.

My head snaps in the direction it's coming from, and in seconds I close in on it. It's partially hidden by rotted food and... I shudder to think of what else.

Standing at the entrance of a narrow alley between buildings, I stare into the darkness. The smell is more potent than it had been on the girl, but it isn't overpowering, as it would be if the vampire were tossed carelessly back in the shadows of this small corner.

My nostrils flare as I inch my way closer. The blood smells too familiar for my liking.

I don't waste another second. I rush to the far wall, my gut clenching in fear.

No... It takes seconds for me to toss all discarded things out of my way.

The fear that had been growing settles and forms into a hard lump in my throat. I reach down and lift a discarded bow and one of the scattered arrows. Dark red blood, nearly black, coats one of the steel tips. My vision blurs as I inhale deeply.

Rosalie. The blood belongs to my Rosalie.

Time loses all meaning as I fight to understand. Rosalie, whose fate I had created by my foolish actions, the only one in this fucked up world I give a damn about. I sink to my knees, not caring about the filth and grim coated ground.

I have failed. My only purpose in life was to protect her. Now her body lies somewhere being desiccated by the local demons. It's far less than what she deserves.

An arrow that smells of Rosalie's blood and the bow that accompanies it has the same distinct woodsy smell as the girl.

My vision fills with red and the wood splinters within my grasp.

I had not intended on returning to that dilapidated structure. The moment I smelled the blood on her, I had not quite believed that she could be capable of such an act. Weak was the first word that came to mind. But the evidence that my assumption had indeed been proved incorrect now lies broken at my feet—both Rosalie's blood and the girl's unique scent were irrefutable.

That slip of a girl will not pay for her crimes at the court's hands but at mine.

CHAPTER
FIVE
CLARA

The fire crackles in our small wood burning stove as Kitty hums to herself on the wooden bench, sewing designs on plain white handkerchiefs. I sit at her feet, rereading my favorite—and only—book for what might possibly be the hundredth time. It's a rare morning where I allow myself the luxury of relaxing and pretending that my life is almost normal.

But only for today. I have every intention of avoiding the woods for as long as I can.

Father bursts from his room, the door cracking against the wall as he stumbles into the room bleary-eyed, hungover, and rubbing at his face. He stops when he sees me, his face turning petulant the second his eyes lock on my face.

"Taking the day off, Clara?" he asks. "Shouldn't you be out there, working?"

I bristle at his tone. He acts as if it's my duty and my duty alone to make sure this family is fed, clothed, and that he has plenty of gambling money to waste.

Kitty's fingers freeze mid-motion, but she doesn't look up at Father. Her nerves are already frayed at the fight that might come. For her sake, I hold my tongue, as much as it pains me to let those words of his go unchecked.

Carefully, I close my book and set it next to Kathrine as I lift myself up to stand.

"I was about to go out," I say as pleasantly as one can through gritted teeth.

His bloodshot eyes narrow on me, not having missed my true feelings. He takes a step forward, his fists clenched at his side, and I ready myself for what's to come.

Three knocks on the door halt him in his tracks. "Don't just stand there, answer it."

Kitty starts to rise. I gesture her to sit back down as I make my way to the door.

I blink several times as I stare into the most beautiful, deep blue eyes that sparkle in the early morning light, made even more striking by the thick lashes that frame them. He's even more stunning in the light. I open my mouth to speak, but my words catch in my throat.

Mr. Devereaux smiles when he sees me, but there's something cold and wicked in it. Today his expression is pleasant in a way that doesn't ring true. Where yesterday he had seemed nearly apathetic, unimpressed... *bored*, today there's malice in it.

My body reacts without thought, moving to slam the door in his face. There's something dark about this man, and I want nothing to do with him.

A red ring forms around his irises, then I blink and it's gone.

Father's meaty hand grabs onto the edge of the door, preventing it from moving. "Mr. Devereaux," he says, frowning. "I hadn't expected you to return so soon... eh—why don't you come in?"

I know what I saw. He is so much more than just a man. Already my mind is forming doubts. A ray from the rising sun flashed just right—a lingering lesser demon causing mischief.

Father's hand wraps around my upper arm, dragging me back out of the way.

Vampire...

No... no, don't let him in!

Father is giving me a murderous look, he will beat me the second this man leaves, but I don't care. My gut is telling me he's dangerous. The two men walk closer to the fire, and I'm left standing with my back against the door.

"I am afraid, Mr. Devereaux, you didn't leave me with sufficient time to gather the funds I owe you," Father says cajolingly, his false pleasantry dripping from his words.

One more punishment I will suffer once our guest has left. I know he will blame me for taking the morning off.

"I regret that more pressing matters have come up and I must leave sooner rather than later." Mr. Devereaux looks at me, taking me in from head to toe, stark hunger in his eyes.

His stare is unrelenting. I feel exposed, even with all my layers of clothes. Once more, the thin ring of crimson flashes around his irises.

Mr. Devereaux wants me to know him for what he is.

He is looking for weakness or fear. If I didn't know better, with the way he holds his shoulders, I would say he's looking to make me cower in his shadow, trying to cow me into submission, ready to be manipulated, and used up... and killed, as though I was nothing more than some dumb animal bred for slaughter. I suppose, compared to them, that's all we really are—a simple and powerless food source.

I can feel his ire as though he were running his fingertips over every inch of my skin. This monster that doesn't know a thing about me has found displeasure in my very existence. It makes no sense. Though, when was a monster ever known to behave or feel logically?

I close my eyes and pull in a shuddering breath and sigh inwardly, careful not to let signs of my fear go any further than thoughts.

My gaze flicks to Kitty then back at him, and I could swear that his eyes sparkle with ill intent.

I glare at him, focusing on calming my breath and slowing my heart to a steady beat. I chase the fear away.

Or at least I tell myself that's what I'm doing. My body has gone cold, chilled to the bone. I only manage to keep my pulse in check due to all those years of practice from hunting, forcing my body to relax so my arrows don't fly too far off target. But vampires aren't mindreaders. He can only sense my physiological responses to him.

He lists his head to the side, and I notice the slight narrowing of his eyes, the corners crinkling. His mouth twitches, not quite forming a sardonic smile.

We stare at each other a long moment before he turns away, facing my father once more.

"Perhaps, when you return this way—" Father tries.

"No." The vampire cuts him off sharply, returning his attention to Father and taking a menacing step toward him. "I will not be back this way for some time, I must collect the debt owed to me and be on my way. I'm sure you can think of something…"

I glance to Kitty, as she keeps her head down, working on her stitching and trying hard not to notice the tension in the room.

"My daughter," Father blurts out, waving a hand toward Kitty. "Take Kathrine, she will make a lovely wife."

"Your—" Mr. Devereaux starts and seems to nearly choke on

41

the words.

"No!" I know I shouldn't interrupt, but I can't allow him to give Kitty away as if she means nothing. I can't allow her to become a meal for one of these monsters.

Mr. Devereaux swivels his attention in my direction, and I know from the curve of his lips before he schools his features that he will accept.

"No," I say again, glad my voice doesn't shake this time. "Not Kitty, she is too young. I will go instead."

The words shock everyone in the room just as much as they do me, but I dare not take them back. I lift my chin as our guest steps closer. He studies me once more with the same look he had earlier, but this time he doesn't attempt to hide it from anyone.

"Not Clara," Father says. "She's—" But he doesn't get to finish.

Mr. Devereaux slices his hands through the air to silence him. "She will do. Our debts are settled."

"Sh-she is worth more than the debt I owe you!"

Kitty snuffles in the corner. I hate this insufferable man. I am used to his hate, his abuse, and every part of his horrible nature. Poor Kitty is not.

His words and his meaning hit home. Kitty isn't worth anything to him, but I am. Not because he loves me, I doubt there's any part of him that knows love—but because I can provide him with money to gamble away.

He disgusts me.

"Mmm, perhaps you are right."

My head snaps up toward Mr. Devereaux. Hope springs in my chest that my initial reaction was wrong. That same hope crashes down around me like so much shattered glass as he reaches within a pocket and produces a pouch, heavy with coin.

"This should cover the difference... and then some. You will find this offer to be more than fair." There's a strange vibration to his words.

Father looks from the pouch to me, then back. I'm frozen in place. No, no. Please, no, I mouth, shaking my head and praying he will refuse.

Kitty looks down at the crumpled handkerchief in her lap. I want her to say something. Anything. Why isn't she protesting?

This entire situation is mad. What sort of man trades his daughter to pay off his debts?

The pouch lands with a clunk on our rough-hewn table. Father's eyes grow wide seeing the size of it. My heart stops for an excruciatingly long moment as he decides. It should be easy.

Refuse! Refuse the damned offer, you bastard! I fling my thoughts toward him, willing him to do the right thing.

I am crushed, though not surprised when Father picks up the bag and extends his right hand. "I find this offer more than fair," Father repeats. "You have a deal."

Mr. Devereaux shakes his offered hand.

43

It is done.

I have been traded for my father's debts. Kitty smothers a strangled sob, but I can't look away from the man who now owns me. I stand in place, my body numb. I can barely remember how to breathe right now. I want to scream and rage and refuse. I want to take Kitty and leave these two to sort out their debts on their own.

The vampire faces me, looking far more devious than he had earlier. "It is time for you to pack, Miss Valmont—we must be on our way."

I stand frozen in place.

"Clara, it is time for you to pack," Father echos placidly. He's looking at me, but it feels as though he isn't truly seeing me at all. "Do not make Mr. Devereaux wait."

Then the vampire turns to Kitty and smiles. Her face goes deathly pale.

I take that for the threat it is and hurry to my room.

My mind goes blank. I can't even think about what to pack. And there is only a single trunk split between Kitty and me. I can't take it with me, leaving her with nothing.

Kitty hurries in behind me. "Clara," she says desperately in a hushed whisper. "Are you really going to let him take you?"

I grab my hunting bag and stuff what I can inside. Two shirts and a spare pair of trousers. I have no room for anything nicer—not that I have any desire to look nice for that beast in the other

44

room. As a last second thought, I shove my hunting knife into my bag and bury it beneath the clothes.

"I have no choice…"

"Clara!" Father shouts from the other room. "What in the Otherworld is taking you so long?"

"Clara," she whimpers. "Do not let that monster bed you." Her eyes focus on the door at my back. "Kill him… Kill him, then return home to me." She clasps my hands pleading.

I am not sure what I'd expected her to say, only that this wasn't it.

I smile and nod as if I'll do just that and be back in a week's time. Though, if I were to kill him, my life would be forfeit. Either way, I'll never see my sweet sister's face again.

"Promise me," she begs again.

"I promise," I say, gathering her up in a tight hug.

CHAPTER
SIX
CLARA

A hand wraps around my upper arm, pulling me away from Kitty, and dragging me toward the door.

"I wasn't finished," I protest, fighting Father's hold.

"You do not need to bring anything at all," the vampire says. "Everything you might need will be provided for you."

I cut my eyes to him, trying to infuse my look with all the disdain I can muster.

Of course, I don't *need* to bring anything. I probably won't make it out of town alive.

"Wait!" Kitty calls out from behind us all. There's an urgency to her voice I never knew possible.

Mr. Devereaux looks expectantly at her, and she hesitates for a second then hurries to Father's far side, trying to put as much distance between her and the vampire as possible.

It's only once she's around Father that I see what was so urgent. My heart plummets. She clutches at my book. And without fuss or another word, she hands it to me before scurrying off to the far corner of the room.

Father shoves me out the door, finally releasing me from his bruising grasp. As soon as the vampire is over the threshold, the door slams shut.

I gape at the weather-worn wood, jaw slack.

He sent me to my doom so easily. I knew he never loved me, but this stings in a way I never thought possible.

"Come, Miss Valmont," the vampire practically purrs my name, motioning to the opulent carriage that awaits us down the long driveway.

Holding back the sting of tears, I turn away from the only home I'd ever known and into the hands of my death.

My legs feel weak with every step. The vampire follows a step behind, one hand out as though he will place it on my lower back to urge me on if I stop.

We reach the carriage in what feels like seconds. The driver stays seated, not once looking back. Mr. Devereaux opens the door for me and once more motions me forward.

I set my bag on the floor inside and climb up on the step. With one foot still on the ground, I pause, gripping the metal handle so hard my skin stings from rubbing the smooth surface. My heart pounds hard against my sternum.

I don't want to get in. I will be dead before we reach the edge of town.

"I didn't get to say goodbye," I mutter. It's pathetic, and I stand to gain absolutely nothing from it. I suppose I say it for my own sake.

"Get in," he says, unsympathetic to my plight.

I spin around so fast I nearly lose my balance. "Where's the chaperone?"

He blinks once and arches a single, dark brow. "What chaperone?"

"The one that should be accompanying us," I say, giving a decisive nod as if this were a common occurrence between us — as if he were a normal man.

"You're stalling."

"I am not." My pulse kicks up.

"I am not," I say. Except I know damn well that I am. My pulse kicks up.

The corner of his mouth ticks up in amusement. "You wear men's clothing and go hunting in the forest alone," he says softly. "Let us not pretend you care at all if you appear proper to anyone."

I hesitate, my eyes darting from side to side, looking around for an escape.

"Get in, *Miss* Valmont, or I will make you," he says with no emotion.

I lift my chin ready to defy him, to force his hand. He takes a step forward.

Turning back around, I get in and sit, pressing myself up against the far side. The interior is covered in black material with a damask pattern and gold flourishes and accents in a simple but elegant style. The seat is cushioned, and possibly the most comfortable thing my body has ever come into contact with.

For a second, I mourn the fact that I have to experience something so grand like this—knowing I'll never get the chance to tell Kitty about it... that I'm going to my death.

He gets in and sits directly across from me, closing the door with a click, and the air within becomes stifling.

"You've made a wise decision."

I scoff before I can stop myself. From his earlier anger, I expect a volatile reaction. Instead, he only leans back, relaxing as the carriage jerks forward.

His stare is heavy, making the silence between us grow thick, I can hardly bear it. I look out the window and watch the scenery drift by. These familiar trees and houses will soon give way to the unfamiliar.

"So am I to always call you Mr. Devereaux, or shall I call you, Master?"

"Why would you assume you will live long enough to call me

anything at all?"

Those few words are enough to take the air from my lungs and the strength out of my defiance—my lack of belongings only serves to emphasize his point.

He removes his jacket and folds it neatly before setting it aside. Somehow, in just his shirt, waistcoat, and immaculately knotted cravat, he manages to look relaxed and severe at the same time.

I don't move, not even to look at him. I only wait. Wait for him to lunge at me and take the only thing monsters like that could want; my blood and my life.

Seconds tick by, bleeding into minutes, then hours. Neither of us speaks until it becomes too much for me to take any longer.

"You're going to kill me." It's not even a question.

"Do you want me to kill you?"

My heart stutters at that. The way he speaks is more casual than he has a right to be when speaking of such things.

My mouth goes dry. "Of course not."

His attention finally relents. I wait for several minutes before reaching for my bag and placing it in my lap. It's another long moment before I start searching, attempting nonchalance.

"If you are looking for a weapon in there, don't bother. I could snap your neck before you made to move an inch toward me."

My hand stills.

He heaves a heavy sigh. "Demon shit," he mutters under his breath.

With lightning fast reflexes, he snatches up my bag with my meager belongings and sticks his hand inside, pulling out my knife. He turns it over in his hand a few times, then lowers the carriage window and tosses it out.

"You can't possibly mean to harm me with such a poorly made weapon." Then he says almost to himself, "You are nothing but a blight on the world. It's as if you were raised by the most bothersome of demons."

"And you're a plague on the world, slowly killing it."

"Miss Valmont—" he starts then cuts himself off. Then, "Miss Valmont. How old are you, exactly? You can't be much more than a child."

His words are like a spark to the tinder of my temper. I know it doesn't matter what I say or do, he will kill me, and I don't doubt that it will be sooner rather than later. I don't see the point in pretending for him.

"Hardly. I'm twenty-one this past winter. And I do not think a child would try to kill a vampire."

"You are right." He eyes me again then says, "You're not a child. Usually, someone of your age would have been married off a few years ago. What defect curses you?"

"Defect?" I ask. The word sounds weak even to my ears. I'm too stunned to process his question.

"Yes, what is wrong with you that you were still living at home like a child?"

"I don't have a defect," I snap. My hands ball into fists.

"Then why were you, a grown woman, still living at home?" he asks again, slowly as if I'm a complete idiot, and he's worried the words he's using are too big for me to comprehend.

My situation is highly unusual. I know it is. I also know that he is only trying to be hurtful, but I bristle at his words anyway even as my heart squeezes painfully in my chest.

Xander and I had always talked about getting married, he just needed to wait for his brothers to marry first so he could choose someone on his own, rather than someone his parents picked for him.

Xander... I'll never see him again, and we were to meet tonight. Now I don't even know if he'll ever find out what happened to me.

I bite down hard on my bottom lip as disappointment settles like a rock in my gut.

But I can't tell the vampire that. It would only lead to his continued mocking, so I settle for another part of the truth instead. "I stayed for Kathrine. She's always been sickly, and someone had to take care of her after Mother was killed."

He regards me for a long moment. I'm thankful when he only shrugs and doesn't bring up the point that our father should have taking care of her. It was thanks to him and his endless gambling debts that I am now the ward—or rather, the future meal—of a vampire.

That is the last we say to each other. I don't know where he goes, but my gloomy thoughts spiral down into further darkness.

I might as well be invisible for all the attention he pays to me, and I am grateful for it. Time passes slowly. My backside hurts, and I grow restless, shifting uncomfortably from sitting in the same spot for hours.

The carriage comes to a sudden stop. I jolt upright and peer out the window. We are still surrounded by trees and the soft sound of rushing water filters in through the carriage.

Eyeing the vampire across from me, I wonder if this is when I become a meal and have my body tossed carelessly to the side of the road.

Mr. Devereaux looks annoyed but doesn't make a move toward me.

I slide across my seat to glance out the window. We stopped just before a low bridge where a family is crossing. The mother hurries to guide her children off and away. Two smaller ones lag behind.

One slips and falls to his hands and knees, rolling around in front of his sister and tripping her.

My heart plummets as I watch the child try to regain her balance, only to fall over the edge.

I don't think. My body reacts on its own. I shove the door open and leap out, breaking into a run and sliding down the riverbank and into the water.

Unholy demon shit, it's freezing!

It's not particularly deep, but the current is moving too fast for someone so small. I dive in, swimming as hard as I can toward the girl, bobbing up and down. Her head going under for longer and longer each time.

Then she sinks beneath the surface and doesn't come back up.

I dip underwater and spot her, caught by an old fallen tree. I reach her in seconds and wrap my arm around her waist and pull her above water.

She coughs and sputters, wildly flailing in my arms.

"I have you," I say, dragging us both to shore.

Her mother is running toward us, the rest of her kids following in her wake.

"Oh, Hanna!" she cries, scooping the girl up. "Thank you, young man."

Young... *man*? I open my mouth to correct her, but she's already hurrying away.

CHAPTER
ƎEVEN
ALARIC

I could have ended her life at any time in the last few hours, yet, I haven't. Doing so didn't feel like an adequate punishment. She deserves worse than to go quietly and in the comfort of this carriage.

Sitting in a confined space with a murderess is a whole new hell. I can feel my fangs start to descend at the thought of draining her tonight.

Perhaps tying her to the back of the carriage and making her walk behind it, for all to see her in her shame would be an improvement.

I run a hand along my jaw. No, that would make her crime too obvious, drawing her into the hands of the court, and out of mine. I would rather rot in the Otherworld than allow anyone to take this vengeance from me.

Her deep brown eyes bore into me, narrowing as the cry of a human spawn vaguely registers.

Miss Valmont swings the door open and leaps out, landing in a full run. For a moment, I can only stare at the space where she sat. She cannot be so foolish as to believe she can run from me.

The shouts from mortals pull me out of my stupor. I exit the carriage and walk calmly to the bridge. I'm not sure what to make of Miss Valmont as I watch her wade into the water, calling out to the child being swept away in its current.

I should jump into the water and drag her back, but I will not allow her to pull me into this charade of hers.

She is little more than a wild animal, feral and untamed, and still, she does this. Her actions don't make sense. Miss Valmont is devious, that is all I know.

My breath catches as she sinks under the surface, following the child's movements. Together they remain underwater for several moments. A woman cries hysterically, her other spawn whimper and wail at her feet as they too watch on.

After a long moment, the top of Miss Valmont's head breaches the surface, followed by the child's, and she stumbles her way to the shore. I wait unmoving until the woman gathers her child, so young, but with long golden locks and glittering blue eyes. My heart goes out to her against my better judgment.

Mud squelches unpleasantly beneath my feet as I make my

way for Miss Valmont at the edge of the water, half expecting her to attempt to run again. Instead, she sits, her legs tucked under her, head bowed, and her hands resting on her knees as water drips from her hair and clothes.

I stop before her, close enough that I could touch the top of her head if I lifted a hand and reached out. She is little more than a drowned rat.

Clara lifts her head slowly. Perhaps I expected fear at being caught, but what she gives me in her eyes is defiance. The wind picks up and she shivers violently.

I put the tip of my finger to my mouth, removing my glove with my teeth, then place it in my pocket.

"Get up," I say, extending my ungloved hand.

Miss Valmont eyes me suspiciously, then, after a moment, slides her icy hand into mine and stands. I move my hand to her lower back, guiding her back to the carriage.

Inside, she sits across from me, eyes downcast, wet hair dripping, and clothes plastered to her body. Each drop of water that falls to the leather seat makes me twitch. It can be replaced easily enough, now that it will undoubtedly be ruined.

She's slight of build, smaller than I'd previously thought with her ill-fitting clothes. Almost fragile.

"Do not attempt something so foolish again."

She drags her gaze up to meet mine. "What?"

"If you try to run again, you *will* die."

"I didn't—" Her jaw clenches. "Am I your prisoner?"

"No," I say reluctantly. "But a debt is a debt, and all debts must be repaid."

The understanding of my unspoken threat shines in her eyes. The fight drains out of her in a soft exhale of air and she slumps back against the seat, shivering and trying to hide it.

She is an enigma to me.

For the life of me I cannot understand her. How can this cruel woman kill one innocent in cold blood, only to turn around and risk her life to save another? One that didn't even have enough sense to learn how to swim.

I'm torn between what to do with her. I should kill her tonight— it's no less than she deserves.

The child, though a pale imitation, reminded me of my Rosalie. And it is that reminder that stays my hand. Rosalie wouldn't want me to kill her. She would want me to let her go, to absolve her of her debt. But I cannot go so far as to do so. I cannot let this crime go unanswered.

Since I learned of Miss Valmont's guilt, I've wanted nothing more than to drain her of her very life force.

But Rosalie would never have approved, not even to avenge her murder. With her kind, sweet nature, she never wanted harm to come to any human. Unlike most vampires, she had kept her humanity since the day she turned, never once wavering. She actually saw humans as our equals.

I have lived my life trying to make her happy, feeding only on those who were willing, and never going too far.

Miss Valmont squirms under my scrutiny.

She hadn't even hesitated to jump in the frigid water when all others, including the spawn's own family, stayed on land and only cried in response, content to lament her fate rather than attempt to thwart it. It is a quality that Rosalie would have cherished.

I am curious to see what she is made of, what other contradictions lay hidden within her.

I feel my will weakening, and I'm not sure I'll be able to kill this girl after all. Not now, knowing she is not entirely heartless, but somewhere down in her dark heart, there lies a shred of humanity.

For now, that is something I shall keep to myself.

CHAPTER
EIGHT
CLARA

Demons take me to the Otherworld now. His constant study grows to be too much, and I fear I may lose my mind before the end of this journey. It's unbearable. His gaze is unflinching and nearly tangible, igniting something down in the depth of my soul.

I shift for perhaps the millionth time. For as luxurious as this carriage is, the cushioned seat still hurts after sitting on it all day long.

He hasn't moved once, at least not in any obvious way. Doesn't he have feeling in his ass anymore, or have too many carriage rides over the years killed the nerves in that area?

If I had thought he might offer me a change of clothes or a blanket when we returned to the cariage, the time I've spen drenched in river water has cured me of that expectation.

I will be provided anything I might need he had told me—it is laughable.

The chill bites and has soaked me to the bone, and I can barely feel my own body, which is made worse by the fact that night has fallen. A dry blanket would be lovely right now. Were I alone, I could strip myself of these clothes as they dried.

Outside, the wind howls, carrying upon it the whispers of lesser demons through the trees bordering the town. A thick fog rolls in, covering the ground in a pale haze.

I turn away, closing the curtain to the window next to me, and look everywhere inside, except at the vampire studying me. My gaze floats around, not finding anything in the simple design to focus on. Everything is covered in black, save for the few gold flourishes, and in the dark, those don't shine. Eventually, I settle on the folds of his jacket.

Being cold is bad enough, but having someone glare at me for hours on end is only adding to my sour mood—even if he has the face of an angel. For the last hour we have circled the town, driving up and down every street, at least once. I'm just about to open my mouth to deliver a derisive comment when the carriage jolts to a stop.

Mr. Devereaux swings the door open and steps out of the carriage, not bothering to look back. He stands there patiently, not moving or saying a word. I suppose it's better than being ordered about like a dog.

After a moment, I step out, my muscles stiff and aching from the cold, and my lack of movement. When I look up, I see we've stopped at an inn, The Grand Manor—though there is little even I would consider grand about it. Two other carriages trot away, having dropped off their passengers moments before we arrived.

Following a step behind him, we enter the inn. The lighting is dim.

The interior is far more beautiful than anything I've seen in Littlemire—wallpapered walls, polished wood surfaces, gas lamps on the walls lighting the inside. Exquisite fabric and décor clutter the sitting room off to our right, and between that and the clerk's desk is an elegantly designed staircase leading up. Then to the left is a set of closed doors. I wonder if it leads to the dining area.

"Keep your head down," Mr. Devereaux says quietly to me.

Instinctively I obey, keeping my eyes locked on the dark, filthy floor as we walk forward to the clerk's desk.

Water drips from my hair and clothes, creating a puddle at my feet. As much as I cannot stand him, I couldn't bring myself to further ruin the luxurious fabric of the carriage by ringing out the water.

I keep my chin tucked to my chest but manage to catch glimpses of the others. The vampires stand in a neat line, each with a human by their side. There are seven claimed humans altogether, but only five vampires, including mine. The humans are all clean, and one woman, little more than a girl, with hair the color of gold dipped in strawberry syrup is even in a pristine white dress—the color of those who actually worship these monsters.

Unlike them, I'm covered in grime and soaked. But I don't regret saving that little girl.

I clench my hands into fists. It's humiliating to look this disheveled and wretched. So I square my shoulders and lift my chin, looking straight ahead. Some of the other humans look terrified, two of them look... happy. My lip curls in disgust.

None of them share a look that comes close to the anger I feel.

The girl in the white dress turns to look at her new vampire master and beams up at him. I think I'm going to be sick. The look of pure adoration is nauseating.

I flick my eyes up at Mr. Devereaux, he's looking straight ahead, a little too interested in the inn keeper's ramblings as he hands out the keys. He's doing everything he can to avoid meeting my gaze.

Standing here, it's all I can do to keep my teeth from chattering. My entire body trembles. If I didn't know better, I would think I was shaking in terror for the life that awaits me, and the painful death he has all but promised me.

Eventually, the vampire at my side is handed a single room key.

I barely hold in my protest. One key. One room. This day keeps getting worse. The only thing I can hope for is that all of us humans will be shoved into a small room while the vampires get their luxurious rooms to themselves. Though deep inside, I know that won't be the case.

Mr. Devereaux turns from me without word or gesture and walks away. He doesn't even look back to see if I follow. My eyes narrow at his back. I have half a mind to stand here until he's upstairs and then just walk right out the front door.

My shoulders slump. Wishful thinking. If I tried to leave, he'd catch up to me before I made it halfway down the street—and that's if the demons didn't get me first—And no doubt I would be slain right then and there. But I've already pushed my luck for today.

Reluctantly, I follow him up the stairs and through the narrow hall.

A few guests peek out through small openings of their door. If he notices, he doesn't show any sign, but I feel the heavyweight of their gazes. Hushed whispers follow us. I try my best to ignore them.

"Vampire whore" reaches my ears in a hiss more than once.

I want to correct them. I want to tell them the truth—that I hate him as much as they do—perhaps even more.

My face burns as I glare at his back. I know he hears the words as well as I, but he makes no move or effort to say anything to the contrary.

Mr. Devereaux stops at the last door in the hall and enters. I stop at the threshold. I can't seem to make myself go further. The room is small and dark. And there is only *one* bed, and I don't for a second believe I could claim it above him. This was a room made for a single occupant.

The thought of being in such a small space with a vampire who commands attention, who seems to swallow up the entire room even when he's trying to blend in with a wall... it will be suffocating just as it was in the carriage.

I think of Xander... he would be furious to see me forced into such a situation.

"Come in and close the door," the vampire orders.

His tone is gentle and soft, almost sad, it throws me off guard. It takes a few seconds for me to remember who I am, remember what he is. I steel my spine and command my heart to harden to stone. Whatever the cause of this sullen state he's sunk into, I will feel no pity for him.

I step through and close the door behind me. It locks with a soft click, but the sound resonates with finality.

A fire crackles in the fireplace on the far wall with a worn lounge chair. To the left is the bed. On the far right wall is an old dusty window with thick drapes pulled to the side to let the moonlight in, and between it and where I stand is a table with a single chair.

This room was definitely made for one person. I expect I will be sleeping on the floor tonight.

The warmth from the fire makes the cold water soaking my skin chill me even more. I stand on just this side of the door and study the vampire's profile as he looks out the window into the night.

Shivers rack my body and, try as I might, I can't control them.

He drags his gaze to me and takes me in. Though his expression is blank, I feel small beneath his gaze.

"Strip," he says.

My blood runs cold.

Demons take me... this is going to be worse than I ever imagined. Worse than him drinking my blood until oblivion swallows me.

"I will not," I snap. I will fight him until I breathe my last breath. If he wishes to kill me, then so be it, but I will not allow him free range of my body.

He sighs and rolls his eyes—the bastard has the gall to roll his eyes at me—then crosses the room in three long strides and grabs my wrist. "You will unless you wish to die from the cold."

With his iron grip, he drags me by the arm to the fire, only letting go once I stand before it. I shiver and wrap my arms around myself. The heat does feel good, but if he thinks I'll strip in front of him, then he is as delusional as he is evil.

A knock startles me. I stay put as he goes to answer it. I peek over my shoulder to see a thin man drag a trunk inside. *He* has a trunk of clothes but couldn't be bothered to let me grab anything.

The two men speak softly, then the door closes. He drags it to the foot of the bed and rummages around for a moment before pulling out a white garment.

He hands it to me and says, "Change into this."

It's not a question or a request but a demand.

I will not spend the few remaining moments of my life bowing to his every whim. I open my mouth to protest but he shoves it into my hand, then spins on his heel and leaves the room.

I wait several seconds, expecting him to return. Then it dawns on me that he left to give me privacy. I lift the garment out at arm's length, and I can feel the blood draining from my face.

It's one of his shirts.

The thought of wearing this feels far too intimate.

Another shiver racks my body, and I decide not to be too picky about it. I quickly remove my wet clothing that clings to my skin and slip the shirt on over my head. It's long for a shirt, coming down just below my butt.

I'm still cold, but the dry cloth feels wonderful on my skin. It doesn't cover as much of my legs as I would prefer. The collar gapes open and shows a good deal of cleavage.

I step toward the trunk, determined to look for another item or two when the door opens. Mr. Devereaux strides in, stopping when he sees me. I flush, knowing I was about to rifle through his personal belongings.

His eyes darken, but he says nothing.

We stand there as he takes me in, and I feel more exposed. I quickly grasp the collar closed with one hand, my other arm coming up to cover my breasts.

I have never been so bare in front of anyone before. Not even Xander. Our hurried meetings were always under the cover of night and never fully undressed.

I move toward the window, as far from the bed as I can get. I sure as hell don't intend on sharing it with him—especially when the look in his eye makes my stomach clench.

He walks past me as I brace myself for a verbal sparring match. He removes his jacket, tossing it carelessly over the chair, and loosens his cravat. I turn my back to him and try to pretend I'm not entirely terrified.

"Are you going to stand there all night, shivering?" he asks from right behind me. "It is like you have no sense of self-preservation." Then under his breath, he adds, "Though I suppose you wouldn't... not to do what you did."

What in the Otherworld is going on... why is he suddenly worried if I'm cold?

He waits a few seconds more, his eyes slightly narrowed. Then he reaches around me and pulls the blankets back. "Get in."

I don't move, and his eyes slit farther.

"What about you?"

"Would you rather sleep on the floor?"

I shake my head and crawl in, covering myself with the threadbare blanket. The mattress is lumpy and uneven, but I don't complain. I turn my back to him. A move I hate because I don't trust him. But I force myself to anyway because I refuse to show him fear.

I hear him on the other side of the room, and I peek over my shoulder. He's laying out my clothes by the fire so they will dry. I quickly turn away, not wanting to watch any longer. The fact that he's doing that confuses me.

I squeeze my eyes tight and snuggle deeper under the blanket. I can't seem to get warm.

Despite what I want him to think, I am still terrified he will drain every last drop of blood from my body at any moment.

Silence fills the room, and once more, I glance over my shoulder. He's standing at the window, staring into the pitch black of the night lit only by the pale crescent moon. He practically oozes melancholy with that sorrowful expression on his face.

I will not feel sorry for this monster. I refuse to be his prisoner — despite his claims that I am not, and as soon as I'm able, I will break free of him, even if I have to kill him.

I try to stay awake, not wanting to sleep, but eventually, my body stops shaking, and the heavy weight of sleep pulls me into its warm, inviting grasp.

CHAPTER
NINE
CLARA

Something brushes my shoulder. I groan, swatting at the annoyance.
It comes again, this time it's a warm hand gripping my shoulder.

"Wake up, Miss Valmont."

My eyes snap open at the deep, warm voice. Then everything
comes back to me.

I'm not at home, not with my sister — I am sleeping in a room
with a vampire who has made no qualms about letting me know
just how disposable I am.

I roll over to my back and look up into dark sapphire eyes,
ringed with red.

Shit. I don't move. The red seems to glow in the dim watery
light. *He needs to feed…*

"Get up and get dressed. We leave in less than an hour."

My breath quickens, bracing my sleep addled brain for what is undoubtedly to come next.

It seems a long moment passes before he turns on his heel and walks out the door. I don't waste a second, scrambling out of the uncomfortable bed.

I pluck up my clothes still spread out in front of the dying fire, and pull them on, moving as fast as I can until I am fully dressed. Only then do I slow, ready for his return. I fold the shirt I wore last night as best I can, trying to get the wrinkles out. A useless waste of time.

I expect him to be back any second, but time passes. I look out the window to the soot-covered town below. The stone of the buildings is dark and covered in patches of some type of lichen. It looks nearly identical to Littlemire, with small differences in the layout of streets and placement of shops.

The edge of dawn slices across the horizon, a thin line of molten gold, stark against the deep blue sky. Demons cry, wailing as they are chased into hiding once more by the sun.

I wait and wait... and wait.

I have nothing left to do, other than to spend time with my thoughts. I had promised Kitty I would kill him and return to her. I had promised myself I would kill him.

Then again, I am dead anyway. I don't know when or how... but I won't let him decide, I will take fate into my hands as much as I'm able.

I look around for a weapon, only finding the fire poker. Not ideal, too large to hide, but I wrap my fingers around the handle anyway.

The door creaks open, and I spin to face him.

Calmly, he closes the door and crosses the room, stopping before me. His gaze flicks to his folded shirt on the chair then back to me. The red that earlier ringed his irises is gone.

"Don't bother."

The way he practically dares me with his arrogant smirk and overly confident words is too tempting to resist. I have killed one of them, and I will gladly do it again, and again, and again until the world is free of these cruel monsters.

I lift my arm and thrust the poker at his heart.

Mr. Devereaux adjusts the cuffs of his sleeves without looking up.

"Stop," he says. His voice is barely above a whisper, but it echoes in my head painfully.

My arm is frozen, outstretched, the iron tip of the poker only an inch away from piercing his flesh. I try to pierce his heart, but my body doesn't move.

What the fuck is happening?

The vampire lifts his head and meets my gaze.

He sidesteps the poker, then slowly, oh so slowly, he lifts a hand and guides my arm to the side. His fingers graze down my arm to my hand. The way he moves is like a dance. Controlled. Graceful.

Swift as lightning he grips the weapon and wrenches it from my grasp, then tosses it across the room where it clanks against the dusty wood flooring.

I can't move. My body is frozen in place, no matter how hard I struggle against this invisible hold.

He takes one step closer, then another, until his chest is mere inches away from mine. I can only stare into the midnight blue depths of his eyes.

The backs of his knuckles graze my skin as he pushes my hair off my shoulder. His fingers splay over my neck from my jaw to my collarbone. With the slightest amount of pressure from one finger, he tilts my head back and leans in.

The warmth from his breath caresses my skin as he draws his face close to mine. I swallow hard, my heart thumping wildly against my ribs. The ruby ring reappears around his irises, and his fangs descend.

His mouth hovers over the crook of my neck, warm breath caressing my skin. I wait for the sting of his fangs to press down.

"You will end up dead sooner rather than later if you do not learn your place." He speaks slowly, his face hovering over mine. I feel his threat down to the marrow of my bones.

His eyes drift lower, pausing on my mouth. I can practically feel his lips on mine and something to coils in my gut at his nearness.

Then he releases me, stepping back. He's looking at me as though I burned him. In a blink, the expression is gone and I'm not sure I imagined it.

He looks at the shirt I slept in, folded on the chair, then picks it up, tossing it into the fireplace as he passes me.

Well, I suppose that makes his feelings toward me more than clear if he feels the need to burn something just because I wore it for a few hours. It's fine with me if I disgust him—the feeling is mutual.

Glowing red flashes in his eyes, circling his irises. In a clipped tone that once again vibrates in my mind, he says, "Come."

My body moves forward, stiff and awkward despite my attempts to fight his command.

"Let me go," I grit through my teeth.

He pauses mid-stride and glances over his shoulder to give me a doubtful look, then keeps walking. *Bastard.*

I stop fighting the force, compelling me to move forward, and my movements become slightly less stilted. I am still his puppet. Mr. Devereaux's hold on me doesn't lessen as we make our way downstairs and outside to the waiting carriage.

After climbing in after him, I expect the carriage to take off immediately, but a few minutes later, a thump of something substantial being hoisted rattles the outside.

My body feels foreign, as though it doesn't belong to me—it's wrong.

"Let me go," I say again, though this time my voice lacks the strength I tried to imbue my words with.

"So you can attempt to kill me again?" he asks.

"Yes," I breathe.

Instead of responding further, he leans back against the seat across from me and closes his eyes.

"What did you do to me?" I whisper.

He doesn't speak or move for a long moment, then he opens one eye and peers at me.

"I compelled you." My body shakes as I struggle against it. "Don't even try to fight it... You can't."

Why do I get the feeling that he has more to say?

Gradually I feel his hold on me loosen. I can move my fingers, my toes, then my legs and arms, and finally, even my spine is mine once more.

I stare at him.

Is he... is he asleep?

He might have removed all weapons from my reach, but he is a fool if he thinks he is safe around me for a second.

Hours pass and the carriage continues at the same pace, even over the worst of the roads—the wheels bouncing in the deep grooves.

I watch the angles of the shadows shorten, then lengthen in the opposite direction as the sun begins to set.

His face has gone slack. He looks far younger right now than when he's awake. A lock of hair has fallen over his brow.

"Don't ever do that to me again," I say eventually.

He blinks open his eyes and looks at me as though he had forgotten I was even here. Then his features harden into the unforgivable mask I am used to. I half expect the compulsion to return to grip me, but it doesn't.

"What did you expect when you agreed to pay the debt? Did you think being beholden to a vampire would be romantic?" he asks mockingly.

"No."

"You're not one of those pathetic worshippers, are you?" he asks with disgust.

At first, I'm not sure what he's talking about, but then I remember the girl back at the inn, red staining the collar of her white dress. I shudder.

"Would you like to be fed upon day by day until you slowly wither away to nothing?" He leans forward, a mixture of seduction and deadly predator.

"No," I say. Only this time it comes out as a whisper.

A sinister smile forms on his full lips. "Unfortunately, what becomes of you at this point has nothing to do with what you do or do not wish to happen. You are not in control of your fate, and the sooner you realize that the better off you will be."

I clench my fists in my lap, gripping the material of my trousers until my knuckles go white. He notices before I can force myself to relax and gives me an unamused look.

"You would do well to learn to control your temper."

"Go fuck a demon," I snap.

The corner of his mouth ticks up as if I amuse him. He leans forward, resting his elbows on his knees, and meets my glare with one of his own.

"You will never win." Red seems to flare in his eyes.

I sit up straighter, determined to not back down. My heart pounds furiously.

He reaches forward and wraps his fingers around my wrist. I'm too stunned at first to rip my arm away. He will feed on me.

Before I can even open my mouth, he says, "Sleep."

That strange vibration to his words scrapes against my mind, and I know he compelled me again. I fight as hard as I can, but still, my eyelids grow heavy, and my body relaxes against my will just as the darkness sets in.

CHAPTER
TEN
CLARA

"Miss Valmont," a distant voice calls to me.

My mind and body feel heavy. I try to stir but can't summon the energy to move or respond.

"Clara? You need to wake up," the voice calls again, this time closer.

I blink up at the pale face hovering above me. It's dark. *Is it already night?*

The face frowns down at me though I can't think of why. I can't seem to focus on who... my eyes drift closed again.

I'm so tired.

My brain is sluggish, my thoughts muddled and scattered.

"I know," the voice says sharply. It must belong to the face.

Is he talking to me? What were we talking about? Where

Something cool caresses my face.

"Clara," the voice says my name again.

This time when I open my eyes, I manage to keep them open. Slowly his features sharpen into a distinct, handsome face. Dark blue eyes, the color of the twilight sky, hold secrets I could never hope to learn, a sharp jaw, and lips that beg to be kissed.

His brows pinch together. He looks worried... *I wonder why.* I lift my hand and press my fingers against his forehead, trying to smooth them, but he catches my wrist.

There's a noise I can't quite make out. Reluctantly, almost as if it pains him, the man lifts his head. "I know. You don't have to keep telling me."

My head lists to the side, though from this angle, I still can't see who he's talking to outside.

When he returns his attention to me, I see a flicker of something. The thought hovers at the edge of my mind. There is a faint sense of familiarity about him.

"Clara, can you sit up?" he asks.

I think about it for a moment before nodding my head. If I actually can or not remains to be seen.

The longer I retain consciousness, the more strength returns to my muscles. I manage to get one arm under me, and he helps support me with my other.

As soon as I'm sitting, he moves across from me.

I take in my surroundings. We're in a moving carriage, the

inside is luxurious but simple. I look from the gold accents to his face several times as things slowly click into place.

Vampire. What in the Otherworld was I thinking? My eyes drift to his lips again before I can stop myself. I look away, focusing on his impeccable cravat. *Is that the same one he was wearing a little while ago?*

"What did you do to me?" I demand, my voice raw and dry. A pounding throbs at my temples from the effort.

"You've been asleep."

Pain so sharp clenches at my middle that I almost bow over. I'm... *famished.* "For how long?"

Just as I think he won't answer me, he says, "Two days."

I look up at him. "Two..."

Now the slightest bit of fear moves in. With one word, he kept me unconscious for two days. He could have killed me... so why hadn't he? And—the carriage is moving.

"When did we start moving again?" I must be more out of it than I thought. I press the heel of my palms into my eyes.

"We never stopped."

I look at him. He is insane if he thinks I'm going to believe that lie. Even in my current state, I know he was talking to someone outside. But it's not important. He can keep his secret. I'm about to say as much when my stomach growls embarrassingly loud.

"Are you hungry, Clara?" he asks, and if I'm not mistaken, he sounds almost repentant. As well he should for keeping me unconscious for so long. I also realize he called me Clara, not *Miss Valmont.*

I eye him suspiciously, not sure how to take his shift in attitude.

"I haven't eaten in over two days... so yes, *Mr. Devereaux,* I am."

Ignoring my anger, he reaches for a small package at his side and hands it to me.

I take it and unwrap it. Inside is a chunk of bread, a few pieces of cheese, and some cured meat. The irony of this situation is not lost on me. He most likely thinks this is the worst meal he could offer up, but I don't know the last time I had cheese or bread that wasn't so stale it needed to be soaked in broth to be edible.

I'm not sure where this came from. Perhaps he stopped while I was unconscious. I take a bite of each and nearly groan. Of course, I'm so hungry that it could be worse and I would still eat it greedily.

When I finish, I am feeling far more myself again.

It's dark. It must be the middle of the night by now. The mournful cry of demons is thick in the air, surrounding us from all sides. I wrap my arms around myself as if that could ward them off.

"They will not harm us," he says, noticing my nerves.

"What about the driver?"

"He, too, will be fine."

I bite the inside of my cheek. There are no lights anywhere outside. We must be miles from the nearest town. "Will we be stopping tonight?"

"No. We will be reaching the estate soon."

The rest of our ride is passed in silence until the carriage pulls up a long, tree-lined drive. I will be glad to get out of this carriage. I feel as though I might lose my mind if I have to spend much more time sitting in this confined space.

The carriage jostles to a halt, then a few seconds tick by before the loud squeal of heavy iron gates sound as they swing open. A few more seconds lapse, then we lurch forward once more.

The trees give way to a large expanse of land with a lake to the south corner of the property. A palatial manor, grander than anything I've ever seen or could have imagined, rises up like a spiny beast against the night sky.

We follow the curve around the massive fountain to the front steps. The doors open, letting out a soft flood of light as three figures, one man and two women, come walking out and lining up the steps, waiting for their master.

The second we come to a stop, Mr. Devereaux opens the carriage door and steps out. He doesn't offer me a hand, and I don't expect one. Not even from someone who comports themselves in a typically gentlemanly manner.

My muscles are decidedly less sore this time. And at least I'm not soaked to the bone in cold river water.

The three figures that had come to greet us stand with perfect posture, eyes downcast, and hands clasped in front of them. He walks up the steps, knowing I'll follow. As he passes each one, they greet him with a bow and a, "Welcome home, Master."

Four servants total, counting the driver... I've never seen so many belonging to one household—one, possibly two, for the most elevated families back home.

I, of course, might as well be a specter, unseen by the living. He doesn't introduce me, and why should he? I am nothing more than a food source for him for whenever he feels like it.

I will count myself lucky if I don't end up in some deep underground layer of the manor, forgotten and left to starve to death.

Inside, most of the candles are not lit except for two candelabras and a handful of single candlesticks... all lit with sweet-smelling wax candles. Not the acrid scent of tallow candles the rich use back home, and not the inadequate rushlights we use.

The floors and wainscoting are all dark mahogany wood, polished to look as if there's a thin layer of glass over it. Area rugs and runners are strewn in just the right spots with intentional perfection. Heavy drapes are pulled to the side along all the windows, letting in the moon's pale light.

It takes me a moment to notice the wallpaper in the foyer, it's a simple cream color with a subtle damask pattern made in glittering threads woven into it that shimmer in the candlelight. The effect is so muted I almost miss it.

I can't tell if he chose something like this because he doesn't care or because he dislikes the bold contrasting colors and stark lines and floral patterns that are so popular.

In the drawing room, a large fire roars, casting warmth and a bit of light into the hall.

He lifts a candelabra and hands me a single candlestick from it. Soft murmurs float toward me as the servants disappear. Except one. I glance at her from the corner of my eye. She hovers a few feet away, barely noticeable, she can't be much older than me.

Mr. Devereaux seems to notice and makes a point to dismiss her as well.

"Follow me," he says, pulling my attention back to him. And there's nothing for me to do other than to oblige him.

We walk through the halls of the manor that is nearly a castle in its own right. For the most part, he is silent, only bothering to point out how to get to the kitchen and a few other rooms. We skip the entirety of the southern wing of the manor.

To my relief, he leads me upstairs to the second floor and not down into some horrid underground place. He passes a staircase and says nothing.

It's pitch black up there, and the light from my measly candle doesn't even come close to piercing it.

"What's up there?" I ask.

He stops in his tracks but doesn't retrace his steps. "That is not for you," he says in clipped tones. "Stick to the places I have shown you. No others, especially up there."

When he resumes walking, I notice two large double doors, unlike any others we have passed.

"What about that room?"

He stops again with an exasperated sigh and looks at the doors as though he had somehow missed them. "That is the library. You may go there..." He looks me up and down. "...if you don't prove to be distracting."

A library. Since I was old enough to read, I've only had the one book, but behind those intricately carved doors lies an endless selection for me to choose from—

I stumble back as something flies past my face and lands on Mr. Devereaux's shoulder.

"What disgusting demon sent creature is that?" I ask, pointing at it.

He frowns at me as he reaches up to stroke its head as it clings to him. It's a bat. It's a fucking bat—small and black with leathery wings and large red eyes—and he's petting it. It chirps and squeaks in my direction.

"Do not be rude, Clara," he admonishes, and I almost feel bad, except it's a *bat—inside—*his house. "This is Cherno."

The creature looks... *hurt.* But that is insane. It's just an animal—and a disgusting one at that.

He resumes the tour, walking a little faster this time, and with the little creature still clinging to his shoulder. He stops once we reach the end of a hall, and without ceremony, he swings the door open and gestures for me to go in.

"This is your room." I look past him into the room. A lazy fire burns in the hearth.

I walk in, and my pulse picks up when he follows. He walks over to the desk up against the wall and sets the candelabra down.

"You will find everything you need in here. Be aware that the servants will not be around after dark." He pauses then crosses the room in a few strides. "Should you require anything else, you will have to wait until morning."

"Why?" I ask breathlessly.

"There are far worse things than I that lurk in the night."

His warning feels like a threat and sends a tremor down my spine. "There's nothing scary about the dark."

He hovers over me, and I think he's trying to intimidate or scare me, but I won't cower.

"The demons that haunt this part of the world are not the weak, lesser demons you know but are the higher demons that will rip you apart."

"Those demons are nothing more than old wives' tales—a way to scare children into behaving. Nothing more than superstitious nonsense."

He circles me, stopping at my back to whisper the words in my ear. "Oh, they are real, more so than your stories make them out to be."

"But with you, I am safe from them?" I ask, remembering how none even came near the carriage on our journey here.

Standing so close behind me, I can feel the warmth of his body. He reaches up and lifts a lock of my hair off my shoulder and lets it cascade through his fingers. "You are not safe with me, my dear Clara. Until you are marked, you will never be safe." He lets his hand fall back to his side, then adds, "and I have no plans to ever mark you."

Don't react, don't react.

Whatever sliver of kindness he had felt earlier is now gone. I spin to glare at him. I know he wants my fear. I agreed to pay Father's debt to save Kitty from ending up in this monster's clutches, I know it means I will most likely die at his hands, but he will not have my fear. I will not let him turn me into some frightened babe.

His words only serve to remind me that I must not forget what I need to do. I must end him.

I cannot forget that he and his kind are the worst evil in this world.

Beautiful but deadly.

And the death of each vampire means more freedom for this world.

Whatever he's looking for in my expression, he doesn't find it. I can see that much in the way his face falls into an emotionless mask.

Apparently, he has nothing more to say tonight, no further threats, because he leaves me standing in this strange room—*my room*—and closes the door behind him with a soft click.

Outside the window, purple bruises smear across the sky as dawn slowly rises on the horizon.

I let out a breath, feeling my shoulders slump as the tension leaves my muscles.

CHAPTER
ELEVEN
CLARA

Three solid knocks on the door have me sitting up, gasping. I scan the unfamiliar surroundings for a threat, and it takes a moment to remember where I am.

At some point, I'd fallen asleep. Even though I'd been forced to sleep for forty-eight hours. Though it might not have been a true sleep but some sort of trance. I could ask him, but I'm not sure he would give me a straight answer.

I can no longer see the sun from my window, but I know it's setting by the reds and orange that streak across clouds, making it look as if the sky is on fire.

The loud knock comes again. I throw the blankets off me and slide out of bed, then hurry across the room.

I open the door only a crack, unsure who will be on the other side.

The young servant who lingered last night. She stands still patiently until she sees my face.

"Dinner will be ready in an hour," she announces curtly and then leaves.

At the mention of food, my stomach grumbles. He can serve me the worst meal he can think of again, and I know it will still be better than what I'm used to.

I look down at my clothes. The same clothes I've worn for three days and slept the day away in. I have half a mind to go to dinner just as I am. What do I care if he finds me repugnant?

But I can't bring myself to do it. I want to be clean for my own sake. Crossing to the armoire, I hope there will be something my size or close enough until I can get my own clothes cleaned and find a way to procure more.

I open it and frown. Dresses. It's all gowns. I reach out to stroke the material of a deep blue dress and stop at the sight of dirt beneath my nails.

A bath first. Even though I can't stand the demon keeping me prisoner in his house, I can't bring myself to ruin such fine clothing.

It takes only a moment to locate the bathing room behind a second closed door. A large plush rug is situated in the center of the room, and beneath it, marble floors gleam. There's a toilet and a washing basin.

Against the far wall sits a porcelain tub that looks as if it's never been used — and *oh demons and saints!* — it even has a faucet. I walk over and turn it on. Working plumbing. And the water that comes out of it is warm.

I quickly plug the tub and only fill a few inches. I feel a sting of guilt at even thinking about filling it, though I would love to know how relaxing that could be.

Carefully I strip, folding my clothes, which are looking all the more filthy in contrast to everything in this place.

Against the far side are shelves built into the wall, holding so many bottles — bottles of perfumes and soaps and lotions and towels and more.

I grab a bar of soap and a washcloth and step into the tub. I sit and nearly slide onto my back, unused to the smooth surface. It's a far cry from the wooden tub I've used most of my life.

Eventually, I find a position where I can wash. The soap leaves my skin feeling soft and smelling of roses.

Once clean, I get out and dry off then wander back into the main portion of the room I'm staying in. I grab the deep cobalt blue dress I had been eyeing earlier and pull it out. I frown, already hating the idea that I'm supposed to wear a corset with it. I wouldn't even know where to begin with the strappy thing.

A quick glance through the rest reveals the same. I've never worn one. And it's just one more detail to make me feel even more inadequate for this place. I wouldn't even know how to lace it up on my own, even if I wanted to.

I'm uncomfortable with how nice everything is. From the carriage, the accommodations here, to the clothes Mr. Devereaux has provided—it's all fit for the elite—and I am a far cry from belonging to a world such as this.

I slip the dress on, forgoing the corset. It fits perfectly, if not a little tighter than I am used to at the waist. Surely, by now, an hour has passed, or close to it.

I open the bedroom door and stick my head out, looking up and down the hall. There's no one there. I think I can find my way, but the tour last night was hurried and not well lit. Everything looks different now in the waning light of day.

I make a few false turns before I pass the library. The doors are still closed, but there's a thin flickering light shining along the bottom from within that wasn't there last night.

I keep walking, only slowing once I reach the staircase that leads to the third floor. The darkness is unusually thick, even now. I feel a pull tugging on me. It's tempting to make my way up there to see what he's hiding.

Now is not the time.

Shaking away the thoughts, I continue on. I need to kill this vampire and be done with it, not skulk around his house looking in rooms with closed doors. This world is overrun, and if I can eliminate one or two, then we will all be better off with fewer of these bloodthirsty monsters hunting us and controlling every aspect of our lives.

After several more wrong turns, I run into the butler. He waits for me in a hall as if he expected me to get lost. He motions for me to follow.

He would be around my father's age if I had to guess, perhaps a little older and in his early forties. His eyes and hair are both nondescript shades of brown, though he has gray streaks at his temples.

When we reach the dining room, he bows slightly at the waist and gestures for me to enter.

"Thank you, Mr. ..." I trail off, not knowing how to address him.

"Steward. James Steward," he says.

"Yes, thank you, Mr. Steward."

He clears his throat, his eyes flicking quickly to the room as if to tell me to stop my stalling.

I pull my shoulders back and breathe, then I enter the massive room.

A long table is situated in the center, with a hearth on the inside wall, with windows along the opposite. A heavy chandelier hangs over the center of the table, tallow candles burning, their light magnified by the countless crystals.

Mr. Devereaux sits at the head of the table, sipping on a glass of port as he reads a book. The place setting before him is empty.

I swallow down my nerves and enter the room. He glances

up briefly before returning his attention to his book. I walk to the only other seat at the table that has been set, and stand behind the chair. I might as well be nothing more than a mote of dust fluttering through a shaft of light for all he sees or cares that I'm here.

With a table as large as this, why was I seated directly to his right? I would have preferred several seats between us.

Eventually, he looks up again and motions to the chair. "Are you going to stand there all day, or would you care to sit and eat?"

That mocking tone of his gets under my skin. Everything I do or do not do is one more thing for him to criticize, something for him to laugh at, something for him to use against me somehow. He has a way of setting my temper ablaze with a few words. It makes me hate him all the more.

I think about refusing to join him out of spite, but eventually, hunger wins out. I sit, folding my hands in my lap.

I'm not sure what to do in a situation like this. I've never been made to dine with a stranger, let alone a vampire. He continues to ignore me for some time.

A woman who I assume to be the head housekeeper walks out from the kitchen. She is older, with her black and silver hair pinned up in a fashionable style. And though she has warm brown eyes, she looks at me with reserved judgment.

She carries a covered plate in each hand, setting one in front of her master, and the other before me, removing the covers in turn.

"Thank you, Mrs. Westfield," he says.

I study him. I hadn't realized vampires ate real food. She pours wine in my glass, and, in an attempt to help quell my nerves, I take a sip of my own drink.

He takes another drink, and it's only now that I can tell that my wine is different from his.

Where mine runs back down the side of the crystal, his lingers. His is thicker, much thicker. Oh demons and saints, my mind swirls as I realize the truth.

It is not wine in his cup, but blood. *Human blood.*

I feel sick. I close my eyes and breathe through my nose before opening them again.

"Are you unwell, Miss?" Mrs. Westfield asks.

I blink at her and nod, attempting to quell her worry with a smile, though I'm sure she can tell it's fake.

Mr. Devereaux finally closes his book and sets it down on the table to his left. "That will be all, Lydia."

"Yes, Master." She bows and leaves the two of us to dine alone.

The food looks and smells fantastic, even despite my recent nausea over the blood. Roasted turkey, potatoes, sautéed vegetables, buttered rolls, and more. I pick up my fork and knife and manage to take a few bites.

"You are a terrible liar. You do realize that don't you?" he says when I've taken my first bite.

I say nothing in response.

He takes a sip of his drink—*blood.*

I wrinkle my nose in disgust. What human had to die to provide that for him? Was it a man? Woman? Child? I shudder and find that I am no longer hungry.

My fingers tighten around my fork and knife as I stare at him. He lifts his own silverware and proceeds to eat the meal before him. Every few bites, he takes another sip.

"It's rude to stare," he says without looking up.

I can't take this anymore, dining with him and pretending that we are longtime friends, or something far more intimate. He's mocking me. Everything about him mocks me.

Kitty's words come back to me again. *"Kill him and return to me."* I had promised her, knowing it would likely mean my own end, but I have no intention of going back on that vow. I'll die knowing the world is a little safer for her.

I stand, shoving my chair back; it scrapes loudly against the wood floor.

"You are *vile*," I say through clenched teeth.

He sneers, he actually sneers at me. His full lips draw my eye. Demons have sculpted this man into some ethereal being. How unfair it is that he's not as hideous to look at to match his terrible nature.

I feel a stab of guilt at finding him attractive. I should find him repulsive to look at.

"Have you always lacked basic table manners? You eat like a wild animal." One corner of his mouth twitches. He is enjoying this—a cat playing with its food right before it delivers the fatal blow and devours it. He slowly stands and mirrors my stance, leaning forward on the table.

My gaze snaps back up to his. I know he's baiting me. I know I shouldn't rise to the occasion, but so rarely does he say anything that is not intended to crawl under my skin and force me to react.

"Kill him... Kill him, then return home to me."

I look down at my hands, gripping my knife and fork so hard my knuckles go white. The candlelight glints off the metal. This elaborate dinner, the accommodations, it's a slap in the face. As if I should be grateful that a vampire is bestowing such luxuries upon me when I'm a lowly human who deserves to fight tooth and nail to just survive another day.

I swing my hand with the knife, slashing at him and aiming for his heart.

His hand moves lightning quick, his fingers wrapping around my wrist, stopping me. The knife never makes it close to his chest. I fight him and use every ounce of strength I possess. My arm shakes, and he's not even struggling. His fingers squeeze, applying more and more pressure until I cry out and drop the knife. The pressure eases instantly, but he remains holding me.

Mr. Devereaux leans forward so I can feel his breath on my cheek.

"That wasn't very nice," he says through clenched teeth, his fangs bared with the slightest hint of blood still on them. His red-ringed eyes lower, lingering on my throat. The tip of his tongue darts out between his teeth, and I'm drawn to the motion. "Dinner is over."

He turns and starts walking out of the room, dragging me behind him. I pull on my arm, but it's no use, and I have to practically run to keep up as he leads me through the manor.

Throwing open the door to my room, he practically throws me inside, only then letting go. I stagger a few steps to catch my balance.

"Do not bother leaving your room until you can act civilized," he snarls.

Then the door slams shut.

CHAPTER
TWELVE
ALARIC

My back presses against the closed doors to my rooms. Black, heavy drapes hang over the windows, blocking the outside world from view. More hang from the four posts of my bed tied back neatly with silken rope.

I fight the urge to find my way back to that infernal woman. I have lost my appetite… no, it's the opposite, it is sparked, and the fact that she is the root of it disturbs me.

At dinner, my gaze had caught on the sensitive patch of skin where her neck and shoulder meet.

I'd planned on making her uncomfortable during dinner—to make her squirm in her chair as she ate each and every bite of her food—I wanted every sip of blood I took from my glass to be a threat so she would know that her blood is next.

It had worked, but she did not fear me. Every word I spoke seemed to set off her temper. And then she had tried to stab me. Her willingness to murder an innocent, and her attempt on my life, as pathetic an attempt as it was, only serves to remind me why I have never taken a human during the claiming before.

To look her in the eye, her expression—she had appeared fearless, but the pulse beneath my fingers, wrapped around her wrist, betrayed her true feelings. The contrast of the two is enticing even now.

I have unknowingly let her into my mind, allowed her space there, giving her the power to make me forget myself and let my hold over my control slip when she insulted me.

She makes an attempt on my life and calls me vile. It was not the word itself, but the venom with which she spewed it that did it. *She* was the murderess. *She* had struck down Rosalie. Rosalie, who would never have harmed a human, no matter how awful.

I wanted to kill Clara, to drain her of every last drop of blood in that dining room... but I couldn't. So many years of living the way Rosalie wanted—it seems as though I am now incapable of the same cruelty as this mortal.

"You seem awfully out of sorts today, Alaric." Cherno flies into my chambers, passing through the wood paneling as though it were only fog, a sealed letter hanging from their clawed feet.

I turn to face the fire blazing in the hearth, choosing to ignore the prying tone.

"What is that you have?"

"Nothing," Cherno says, flying farther across the room. "Tell me, Master, about the girl."

"There is nothing to tell, so hand over the letter." I cross the room, intending to snatch it from the little imp.

Cherno flies higher out of reach, large red eyes growing wide, a pout on their furry little mouth. I groan, knowing I've lost the battle.

"She infuriates me," I grind out the words unwillingly. "Claiming her was a mistake."

Cherno lets out a snort. "From one insult? I would have thought you would be impervious to that sort of thing by this point."

"You were at dinner," I say flatly. "Why must you insist I tell you about it?"

A smile. *Damned demon sent bat.*

They fly to the chandelier in the center of the room and hang upside-down, holding the letter in their tiny, clawed hands.

"She killed Rosalie."

"So you have said..." Cherno hums thoughtfully. "But barring that, perhaps there is more to the situation. After all, if revenge and hiding from the court was your goal, then why does she still live?"

"That is the only thing that matters," I snap.

"You knew this fate would come to Rosalie sooner or later." I flinch at the truths they speak. "There are a number of humans that would see all vampires killed, and Rosalie made herself vulnerable to mortals. Her heart was too soft to resist them."

I stare into the fire, watching the flames as they dance. "I don't know what it is about her that gets to me," I admit quietly. "She is nothing like I expected."

"You are used to humans cowering before you in fear or worshiping you. She does neither. Perhaps that is why you find yourself drawn to her."

"Do not make me kill you, bat. Because I will if you continue to spout such nonsense."

Cherno drops from the chandelier and flies around the room in quick erratic movements, laughing with childlike glee. "We both know you would never harm me."

I glare at them, but the effect is lost by the smile that forces its way across my mouth. "I wouldn't, but do not push me, or I might change my mind."

Landing on the fireplace mantle, the envelope dangles from Cherno's feet. I recognize the seal, and suddenly, I have no interest in the contents of the letter within.

"You should get to know her."

"Clara? Why should I waste my time? She will be dead soon enough." I pace the room feeling restless in this space but not trusting myself to leave my room just yet.

"Because you call her Clara and not Miss Valmont."

I stop walking. "I brought her here to make her life hell for what she did, not to befriend her."

Cherno takes to the air once more, hovering before me only the way a bat can. "Do not be so arrogant as to think there is no other reason for your paths to have crossed."

Demons free me from this cursed beast. I narrow my eyes. "Shouldn't you be watching her? And take the letter to the study."

"You don't wish to read it?" they ask, flying near the fire. "Perhaps I shall burn it for you instead?"

"No, you mischievous demon. As much as I would love that, I will... read it later."

With a grunt, Cherno flies off the way they came.

CHAPTER
THIRTEEN
CLARA

It's late. It must be nearing midnight by now. I know because the demons of the forest beyond the property line sing their melancholy song. The moans are louder now than when they wake and even louder still than the hours before dawn.

I pace the room waiting for the vampire to return and kill me for what I attempted at dinner.

It was brash, unplanned, and sloppy. I should know better when dealing with a vampire such as him. I can't allow my anger to control me if I want to have any hope of killing him. I am either lucky, or he has something truly terrible in store for me.

In either case, I should have a weapon ready. Though there

nothing in this room that I can use.

My hand hovers over the doorknob with a slight tremble. He had bared his fangs, but it wasn't until he dropped his eyes to my neck that I'd felt as though I were in danger. Before that, there was a different kind of hunger in his gaze.

I'm not his prisoner. I'm not his prisoner. He gave me free rein of most of his manor.

I pull open the door and step out into the hallway before my nerves get the better of me. All is quiet as I exit the room.

Though I was never forbidden to leave my room, a trickle of unease slithers down my spine, but I press on.

My feet take me to the library as if by instinct. The doors are carved with beautiful roses and vines, the contrast of the two beautiful and deadly. I have lived most of my life with a single book to read over and over again, and just a few steps beyond where I stand, endless worlds await.

I glance over my shoulder, down the hall toward the staircase that leads to the third floor. The shadows beckon to me.

What dark secrets are hidden up there? I make my way to the foot of the stairs and pause with one foot on the first step.

I shouldn't… it is the only place he strictly forbade me to go.

One step after another, I climb the stairs until I reach the top. There are only three doors on this floor. I walk up to the first and hear a single voice murmuring. It must be Mr. Devereaux.

Who could he be talking to?

I had not realized anyone had come by so late.

For half a second, I fear it must be another vampire. If that's the case, I need to find a weapon to defend myself or kill them with. The next room is closed and pressing my palm up against the door, it's cold, as though it has not been opened, nor a fire lit within for days.

The third door at the end of the hall is cracked open. I make my way over to it. There's something about it that seems like this is where I was meant to go all along. But that's crazy.

Looking through the small opening, there's a fire going, but no movement or sounds, save for the crackling of flames as they consume the logs of wood.

I squeeze my way through and close it most of the way.

It's a large office with two dark leather wingback chairs, a mahogany desk, and shelves of books and artifacts along the walls. A large area rug covers the majority of the wooden floor.

There are a few things scattered throughout the shelves in a deliberate fashion; a marble bust of a woman, a porcelain vase, and a clock.

On the opposite side of the fireplace are more books, with one shelf devoted to a decanter filled with a dark amber liquid, with three crystal glasses encircling it.

Continuing to make my way around the room, I look out the window. Below is a large field, but up against the house is a massive conservatory made of frosted glass and iron framing crafted into beautiful geometric shapes.

I move on to the large desk. There's an oil lamp, some stationary, and a quill set next to an inkwell. And upon the center of the desk is a letter. Skirting the desk, I stand next to the chair, skimming my fingers over the name on an envelope. My finger traces the loops and swirls of the practiced and elegant lettering. There is only one name printed: Alaric.

Is that his name? I turn it over in my mind, picturing his face when we were in the carriage, and he had fallen asleep. It suits him.

On the left side of the desk is a sheathed, stiletto dagger. Roses and thorny vines twist around the handle with the same motif that graces the library doors. Slowly, I reach for it. My fingertips skim the metal expecting it to be cold, but it's almost warm to the touch. This is precisely what I need. I quickly stick it in the pocket of my dress, making sure it's hidden.

I feel a rush of a breeze at my back, causing the ends of my hair to flutter. A hand wraps around my upper arms and spins me around so fast I lose my balance. By the time my world rights itself, I'm pinned against the desk, Mr. Devereaux's arms caging me in.

He leans forward, a lock of unruly hair falling across his forehead. His musky, masculine scent fills the air between us. Heat pools in my lower abdomen. I squeeze my legs together, trying to stifle my reaction.

"What are you doing in here? I told you this floor was off-limits."

I can't think with him this close.

"I-I'm sorry," I say. "I didn't mean any harm, I was just..."

"Disobeying me? Spying on me? Tell me, Clara, why, out of every room—every section of this manor—do you chose to go into the one place where I asked you not to?"

He leans closer. I can smell his soap on his skin. I lift my chin and tilt my face away, unable to continue to meet that piercing blue gaze.

It's then I realize my mistake. He leans in further, lowering his mouth toward my neck. His warm breath brushes against my skin, sending a wave of heat through my veins that settles in my core. I squeeze my eyes closed and wait for the sharp pain of his fangs.

But he's drawing it out. The anticipation of the pain is almost worse. I know he can hear my pulse pounding wildly in my veins. I lift my hands and grip the material of his sleeves.

He drags his nose from the base of my neck to my jaw to my earlobe.

"Alaric... please," I say breathlessly. My heartbeat roars in my ears, nearly deafening me.

He freezes at that. And for a long moment, neither of us moves. Then slowly, he draws back, guiding my chin, so I have no choice but to meet his gaze. Just as I expected, crimson circles ring his sapphire irises.

"How do you know my name?" he asks quietly.

I lick my lips, my mouth suddenly dry. His gaze follows the movement.

"Th-the letter. I saw the letter."

The hand that had guided my head still lingers on the side of my neck. He is going to kill me this time. I know he will, and I don't even have the leverage to grab the dagger and unsheathe it to defend myself.

"Do you alw—" he starts, but I don't let him finish.

I jerk my head forward, slamming my forehead into the bridge of his nose. He takes several steps back and grabs his face where I made contact.

While he's stunned, I bolt from the room, knowing he'll be on my heels in seconds. I leap down the stairs, taking as many at a time as I can without tripping over my skirt.

By some miracle, I make it to my room and slam the door closed. Backing up to the center of the room, I snatch the dagger from my pocket and pull it from its sheath, clutching it in my hand as tightly as I can.

And then I wait.

I listen in the spaces between my breaths and wait for him to pound at the door… for him to break it down and force his way in, and finally end me.

But as my breathing and heart rate slow, I realize he won't.

CHAPTER
FOURTEEN
CLARA

Dawn is breaking, and the gray light of morning leaks in through the window. I am alive, but I don't for the life of me understand how.

I sit at the head of the bed with my back against the cool wall, my knees pulled up to my chest, still clutching the dagger. Waiting. Waiting, waiting, waiting for the vampire to burst in my room to attack me while I sleep.

So I didn't allow myself to sleep, and now my eyes are heavy and dry.

I hadn't even come close to killing him at dinner last night. It was as if that insufferable man knew what I was going to do before I even moved. I must learn to be stealthy.

What have I done? What have I done? What have I done? The question repeats over and over and over until it drowns out all other thoughts. What had possessed me to agree to go off to live with a vampire and leave Kitty and Xander? It was the most foolish thing I've ever done...

And yet, I would do it again to save my sister from this fate. Though somewhere over the past few days, I've let my arrogance — and my promise to Kitty — cloud my mind. That vampire I killed in the forest... that had been nothing more than ideal timing and plenty of luck. It hadn't seen my arrow coming, hadn't realized I was even there.

Mr. Devereaux must know by now that I have every intention of fighting him when he does come for me.

But now that I am here... who will take care of poor Kitty? My decision to take her place was too hasty, leaving her in Father's incapable hands.

Somehow, I need to find my way back to my life.

Uncurling myself, I drop my feet off the edge of the bed, and, eyeing the door, I reluctantly set the dagger down on the table next to the bed. I run into the bathroom and look for my discarded clothes from yesterday. Gone. One of the housekeepers must have taken them while I was at dinner last night.

Turning around, I return to the main room. I might as well check the armoire to see if there is anything I can possibly use.

Nothing but an assortment of dresses and corsets.

Forgoing the corsets all together, I unlace my dress. It falls to the floor in a heap of silk and lace. I pick out another, attempting to find the least cumbersome one.

I smooth my hands down the sides of the dress. These clothes cannot last, they are far too nice for someone who is a meal.

I grab the dagger from the night table, sheathing it, and strap it to my leg. It's not ideal by any means, and the skirt could pose a problem. It's all I have for right now and still relatively easy to grab.

No hesitation.

I stride out of the room and down the hall, ready to face the vampire.

Making my way through the halls, I come across the butler, Mr. Steward. He carries a silver tray with an empty glass still tainted red with blood. He says nothing, but I can feel him watching my every movement as we pass.

Everything looks like it had been cleaned moments before. The entire house has the feel of being busy, but almost always just out of sight. I've only ever seen three of them, but for a house this large, surely there must be at least half a dozen more.

I get to the front end of the manor and hear the clattering of dishes coming from the dining room. I stand in the doorway, staying hidden from whoever is inside and press my back against the wall. After a few heartbeats, I slowly look in. Two slender hands belonging to a woman are arranging various dishes and cutlery on the table, and the soft murmur of feminine voices.

I glance around the large dining room, wary that Alaric might be near.

"Are you looking for something, Miss?" The young servant from yesterday asks. Her red hair has been pulled back into a bun at the nape of her neck. She smiles warmly and looks at me expectantly as she waits next to the dining table with the head housekeeper dressed in the same uniform.

"No," I say slowly as I step into the room. There's only one place setting.

"He's out, Miss," Mrs. Westfield says.

My gaze drifts back to hers as I quit skulking and walk up to the nearest chair, resting my arms along the back. Her voice pulls me out of my thoughts. "He? Oh, you mean Al—Mr. Devereaux?"

The two women look sideways at each other.

"Yes, Miss." The younger clasps her hands in front of her. "Will you be having lunch?"

Both of them assess me from head to toe, and if they suspect my motives for inquiring about Alaric's whereabouts, they won't hesitate to inform their master.

I feel the tension leaving my shoulders. He's not here. I am half relieved I won't have to confront him now. But also in that same breath, disappointed.

The older housekeeper lifts the silver dome cover and reveals a plate of sausages, boiled eggs, potatoes, pork, and bread with a side of jam. It seems a little over the top.

I eye the meal. I have never had such a feast for my morning meal. I might as well take advantage of it while I can. I don't plan on staying here for long.

"Yes, thank you, Mrs. Westfield," I say.

"You're welcome, dear, but please call me Lydia," she says with a smile. It's almost a warm expression, but her eyes are slightly too narrowed to be genuine. She dips her head then turns and leaves through the door that leads to the kitchen.

The younger is still watching me. I lift my brows, not sure what to call the girl who can't be much younger than I am.

"Elise," she offers.

"Thank you, too, Elise." She turns to go, but something occurs to me. "Elise?" I say. She stops and tilts her head, inquiringly. "I do have a question."

"Yes, Miss?"

I breathe in then let out a breath. "Why is he treating me like this?" I motion to my dress, then the food on the table that is fit for someone far more important than a poor girl from a nothing town. "When will I..." I frown, not quite sure how to put this without being rude. "When will I become his... *servant?*"

"You are his guest, Miss," she says, frowning.

I scoff and glower at the plate of food, the rich aromas waft up and tempt me. "I am not a guest—I am a possession."

"If that is what you think, then you are mistaken. And we are not his servants—we are his hired staff. The others have come to him seeking employment. I was born into it, my parents worked for him until they died, then he was kind enough to take me in.

Now, if you'll excuse me, I have other duties to attend to."

She bows curtly then leaves me to sit and dine.

I stare dumbly after her, shocked by her outburst.

That vampire must have compelled them all into loyalty...
though when he compelled me, my body was under his control,
but my mind was still my own.

When neither woman returns, I sit and dig into my food. With
the first bite, I groan. This food is delicious and decadent. After
another few bites, I shovel it into my mouth, barely finishing one
before I take another, washing it down with tea sweetened with
sugar and a splash of milk.

"Miss?" Elise says from the doorway.

I nearly choke, not realizing she had reappeared. Her placid
expression has returned.

Demon's tits, she's quiet. I put the silverware down and lift my
glass to my lips, taking large gulps.

"Do you need anything else, Miss? More tea, perhaps?"

I push back my chair and stand, swallowing the last bit of
food. "No. I don't think I could eat another bite. Thank you for
the meal."

I skirt the table and pass her and head toward the front entrance.
Elise clears her throat, making it obvious she has something more
to say. I stop to look back over my shoulder.

I smile for her, pretending that everything is fine, but it's
strained and already making my face ache with the effort.

"Miss, if it's all right, I would like to ask you a question."

I nod.

"Earlier—" She plays with the hem of her sleeve, hesitating for such a long moment that I'm not sure she is capable of finishing. "—why did you assume you would be..." her question trails off.

I say nothing. She is an idiot to not realize what it means when a vampire takes a human during the claiming.

"Do you not like the Master?" Elise whispers the question.

"No, I do not," I say before I can stop myself.

Elise wrinkles her nose as if it were abnormal to loath a thing that fed on you. Even rabbits know that the fox is not their friend. It is all too clear that she adores the beast that keeps her. Poor thing.

Her mood shifts visibly across her pale face.

"He has been nothing but kind to you. He allows you to stay here, feeds you the best food—" Once more she takes me in from head to foot, only this time she looks as if she smelled a pile of horse manure. "He gives you the best clothes."

"Then you don't know him as well as you think you do. You don't know what he's done."

"The only thing he has done is improve your life."

She's angry again. But so am I. Elise is a fool if she thinks being given clothes, a large room, and pretty things is enough to make someone worthy of adoration—for ripping me away from the ones I love and the life I have fought tooth and nail for.

"You have no idea what you're talking about," I say, turning my back on her. "It takes more than material possessions and money to win someone over."

"I know he is a good man."

Otherworld take me, this girl is crazy. *A good man?* She is so deep into her delusion there is no use trying to explain how much he falls short of that mark. The other servants must be equally blind to who and what he is as well.

"I'm going for a walk," I say. I storm from the room and out the front door, effectively ending the conversation.

Once I get outside, the cool air takes the edge off my irritation. I make my way through the gardens. White gravel crunches underfoot. I wander through the paths, between rows of rose bushes and shrubs. Occasional birdbaths decorate where the pathways intersect.

I stop at a bench beside a small circular pool of water with a blanket of lily pads over half of the surface. The stones placed around it start small and gradually get wider as they fan out. Green moss grows thickly in the grooves. I plop down on the bench and grip the edge with my fingers and wait for my anger to dissipate.

The next several days pass quietly in the manor. I could almost believe Alaric has left for good. I haven't seen him in a few days. Except I do spot that flying beastie of his hovering around me in my wanderings.

It still surprises me that Mr. Devereaux has not come for me or taken back his dagger. I have managed to sew pockets into most of the dresses in my wardrobe to better hide it.

I have returned to the small pond every day for the last three days to think, and it is today that I have decided...

I will kill the vampire tonight.

Though it's something I have been telling myself I would do since Kitty asked it of me, I hadn't thought of what it would truly cost me. Kitty.

And so I am finally ready to give up the life I have planned and waited for. I must be prepared, or my attempts will amount to nothing but angering him, and I will die accomplishing nothing.

If any vampire finds out I've killed him, it will mean instant death. But I have seen neither hide nor hair of any other vampires since he brought me here. And while there is an extra room on the third floor, none of the staff has ever mentioned any visitors, nor did Alaric when he gave the tour. The only warning he gave was of demons.

I imagine sinking this dagger into his heart and what it would mean.

The three servants would be free, no longer forced to pretend to love him.

And I will be free.

CHAPTER
FIFTEEN
CLARA

"Ouch," I hiss through my teeth and suck on the tip of my finger.

Demon shit, that hurts.

It's the twentieth time this evening I've pricked my finger sewing a pocket into this dress. My back aches from doing this all day. I only have a few more to do, and then no matter what I choose to wear, I will be ready for him. Kitty was always the better seamstress between us. She had the patience and grace for this kind of work.

A gentle knock on the door startles me.

"Who is it?" I ask. *It's the housekeeper.*

And sure enough, Mrs. Westfield's voice calls sweetly through the door. "Miss, the master requests your presence in one hour for dinner."

A thrill runs through me. I'm silent for a long moment. *Alaric is back?* The thought of being around him again ratchets up my pulse, and my nerves hum.

"Miss, did you hear me?"

"Y-yes, thank you!" I call. "I will be right there."

I have been waiting for this moment. A fact I now need to remind myself of.

Setting down the sewing, I run my hands up and down my arms, trying to regain some warmth.

I waste no time in putting on a clean gown and running a brush through my hair, I have no talent for creating a fashionable style, so I opt for something simple. As a last-second thought, I even dab a little perfume on my wrists and neck, going with one of the lighter scents. It smells of warm amber and jasmine.

There's something perverse about trying to look as appealing as possible for a man I intend to kill.

Once I finish getting ready, I stand before the door. I inhale a single breath, hold it, then slowly release it. I reach again for the handle of the dagger in my makeshift pocket then smooth down the sides of the blue silk dress. Delicate lace accents adorn the edges, and the cut of the neck is straight, leaving most of my chest and shoulders bare.

My fingers grip the hilt of the blade then release it. I am outmatched in all ways, but I will wield my claws in every way

I can.

I hate what this horrid dress symbolizes, that it is one of the most exquisite things I've ever seen, let alone touched, and it's because of that vile beast waiting for me. A monster that would kill my sister and I for sport, just like one did our mother when we were barely old enough to understand.

Squaring my shoulders, I banish thoughts of the past from my mind. I must focus on my task.

With that, I open the door and stride out of the room. As per usual, the halls are void of the three servants that live here. The sun is setting, so I don't expect I'll be seeing them until morning.

I pause at the entrance to the dining room. He sits in his usual spot, reading. As soon as I step one foot into the room, he folds the newspaper and sets it aside. His plate is still covered. He was waiting for me.

He lifts his glass and takes a sip of the thick red liquid.

He is painfully beautiful. More so than I remember... and it's only been a few days.

I swallow my nerves and stride over to him, keeping my eyes downcast. *I can do this. I can do this.*

My hand presses tightly to my side against the handle of the dagger. He stands when I stop before him and not at my chair.

"You came," he says. If I'm not mistaken, he sounds almost surprised.

I inhale deeply.

"I'm sorry," I say, and the words taste foul in my mouth.

He's silent for so long that I start to think I only thought them instead of speaking them aloud.

"For what, exactly?" he asks doubtfully.

"The other day."

He hums as though he's weighing my words. Then, "No."

"No?" I ask, finally lifting my head to meet his gaze.

"No, I don't believe you are. Come now, Clara, we both know you would rather see me dead than standing here before you. Yet you would have me believe this blatant lie," he says. He stands slowly to lean over me.

My anger wends its way through my veins, and it's all I can do to keep it tempered. He's right, but it still infuriates me.

I clench my hands into fists, my nails dig into the sensitive skin of my palms. I don't speak. I can't, not without striking.

"That is an impressive feat without a corset," he murmurs, and my eyes snap to his face.

"What?" I ask. *Did he...* my face burns and I am entirely disarmed at the implication of his words, and with them, my resolve comes undone.

I raise my hand and swing, aiming for that smooth, flawless face. I blink and he catches my wrist in his hand. His gaze travels up my neck to my face, a crooked smile forming.

My breaths come out short and quick with my rising anger. I grab the dagger with my other hand and thrust it at him, but my hand doesn't get any higher than my waist. I fight his hold over me, my arm shaking with the effort. Finally, I plunge the blade into the table between us.

"Are you going to make an attempt on my life every time we have a meal together?"

He is already so close, but he closes the distance between us until our chests are all but touching. His warm breath brushes over my face. I glower at his perpetually bored expression. His gaze flicks to the dagger then back.

"Do you know the cost it will take to repair that?" he asks flatly.

"Threaten me all you like, Mr. Devereaux, I will never be afraid of you."

His head lists to the side as a single dark brow rises in question. "I did not threaten you. If anything, it is you who has murdered my poor, defenseless table." Finally, he moves away and goes to stand in front of the fireplace. "Were you trying to kill me as you promised your sister you would?"

I blanch. He wasn't in the room when I made that vow to her. He couldn't possibly know that...

But he does.

I don't bother trying to deny it. "I had to give Kitty hope that I would escape."

Alaric stops pacing, his chin raises a little higher to look down on me as a sneer forms across his lips. "You come to me as though you are some poor victim of circumstance, but you are not."

Tears of frustration well behind my eyes, burning, but I refuse to let them fall. "You know nothing of my life. A monster like you could never hope to understand what I have gone through."

The anger fades from his face, leaving behind neutrality. "Monster?" Alaric tsks. "You wound me, Clara. That is not a very nice thing to say after all I have done for you. Have I not been kind?" He takes a step closer. "I have fed you—" Another step. "Clothed you—" Another step. "Given you shelter far superior to anything you could have ever dreamed... and yet you still call me a monster?"

I don't answer.

"Tell me, my dear Clara, what I have done that is worse than what you are guilty of?"

Taking me from my family. Threatening to kill me. Being a vampire. I open my mouth to say as much, but instead I say, "I don't care about possessions, and I don't care what my father owes you. Settle his debt with him." I drop my gaze down and to the side, unable to look him in the eye.

"My dear, Clara..." He lifts a hand and strokes my hair. "Do you think I give a shit about your father's debt to me? That man could have won a hundred times that amount from me and it wouldn't have made a dent in my coffers. This was never about him... it was always about you."

"I've done nothing. I am innocent." I try to give my words strength, to keep my fear and confusion from surfacing, to dare him... but they come out soft and weak.

Alaric's eyes darken as I speak. "Is that what you think you are?" He now stands only a breath away. "Innocent?" he spits out the word.

"Yes," I breathe.

He chuckles darkly but there is no humor in it. "We both know that is not true. I think it is time you tell me what you've done."

"I haven't done anything," I insist again, and I almost believe it myself. "I am innocent."

"Don't lie to me," he snarls.

I narrow my eyes. I refuse to give in to him.

His lip curls. "I gave you a chance, but it seems you would rather have me force it from your lips."

I back up until I am pressed up against the table.

His hand lashes out, grabbing the back of my head, his hold forcing my face closer to his. For a second I can't tell if he's going to kiss me or bite me.

But he does neither. His eyes flash then darken.

"Tell me," he whispers deadly sweet. The words echo through my mind and my body becomes numb and pliant in his hands. "What you did that day in the forest."

My eyes grow wide. Black fills the edges of my vision until

his face is all I can see.

I feel his power slide over my skin like a caress. It slips past my lips and down my throat. I fight with everything I have against it. But the words form on my tongue as if I want to say them.

"I killed a vampire." The confession is ripped from my mouth.

"Tell me about the vampire."

"It was a vampire. Just some weak, low power vampire."

"Was it self defense?" he demands as if he already knows the answer.

I whimper. Trying to fight, but it's useless, my body is not my own. A single hot tear rolls down my cheek.

I fight against the pull of his compulsion, but it's no use. "No."

"No... *what*?"

"No, it wasn't self-defense. She was eating a... rabbit."

"Then why did you do it?"

"Please..." I choke out.

"Why did you do it, Clara?" he purrs my name.

"Because there are too many of you. You hunt us. Steal us. *Murder* us..."

He releases me, and I feel his power slip from me like water sloughing off.

I feel empty. My mind and mouth have betrayed me, and even still his power lingers like the caress of a lover.

"I hate you," I rasp out. My knees give out, and I slump to the floor.

Alaric kneels before me, smiling. Then his face goes hard and stony, his fangs glinting in the firelight.

"Make no mistake. You are alive only because I wish it to be so. I could kill you before you took your next breath if I felt the whim. If something should happen to me, there are plenty of vampires far worse than I who wouldn't hesitate to take my place." He pulls away, releasing me roughly. "Your death at their hands would be infinitely worse than anything I could give you."

My breath comes in short, quick bursts. The adrenaline running through my veins makes it hard to even my breathing. My mouth is as dry as cotton.

His words are muffled, his face blurs before my eyes.

I can't catch my breath.

He reaches for me as darkness moves in.

CHAPTER
SIXTEEN
CLARA

I wake in my room, sitting up with a start… and instantly regret it. My head swims, aching, and foggy. I press a palm to my forehead in an attempt to stifle the pounding.

What happened?

One minute, Alaric and I were fighting and then… and then he was compelling me—forcing the truth from my lips.

I slide my legs off the edge of the bed and freeze when I see the dagger lying on the top of the night table. Taunting me.

It's a threat. A dare for me to try again.

I stand. My legs are still weak, but I force them to steady. Grabbing the dagger, I storm out of the room, determined to find him and let him know that I still don't fear him. His tactics will not work on me.

After a minute, my pace slows. I pant from the exertion. For once, the doors to the library are open wide, but among the vast shelves of books that reach from floor to ceiling, a few chairs, and an unlit fireplace, there seem to be no signs of life within.

I take a few steps inside, enthralled by the sheer number of books. There are more books here than I could ever hope to read in my lifetime. The idea of reading something other than the book Mother gave me is both intimidating and thrilling.

On the far right is a dark mahogany spiral staircase leading to a catwalk that is halfway up the wall. This room spans all three floors. Rain beats against the windows that span almost as high.

I want to run my hands along the spines of the books, to pull each of them from the shelf and flip through the pages, devouring each and every word while inhaling the smell of ink and paper and leather binding.

"You are awake," Alaric's voice says softly behind me.

I nearly jump out of my skin as I spin to face him. It is one of the few times he's not scowling or raising his nose to look down on me.

His dark hair is mussed as if he spent the last hour running his hands through it over and over. But the rest of him is immaculate, from his dark trousers, his freshly pressed shirt and black vest with intricate gold brocade, to his neatly tied cravat.

I nearly forget myself as I look at him in the dim light, the pattering rain against glass is the only sound for a long moment.

"How are you feeling?" he asks, attempting to approach slowly.

How do I feel... he means after he compelled me. And with that thought, my anger has returned.

"I am fine," I bite out, "no thanks to you."

He flinches slightly at that.

I stomp toward him, letting my fury give my legs the energy to move quickly. I shove the point of the blade toward his face. I expect him to stop me, to take the dagger, or step away. But he doesn't move. The sharp point nearly touches the underside of his chin.

"You are threatening me with this, and it won't work."

Alaric lifts his hand and wraps his long, elegant fingers around my wrist, gently guiding the dagger away. "Am I now?"

"Yes!" I say. "It doesn't matter how many times you compel me or threaten me—I will never be afraid of you."

"And is that why you were searching for me, to tell me this?" He tugs on my wrist just enough to throw me off balance. I am forced to take a step to keep from falling into him. "Are you sure you're not here for... *other* reasons?" he asks, his tone full of meaning that makes my blood heat.

His other hand settles on my waist, and he pulls me closer until my front is flush against his. His eyes are focused on my mouth, then they lower.

I follow his gaze to my dress... but it's not the dress I put on for dinner. It's a nightgown. I had been too set on finding him to realize someone changed me.

"Did—did you?" I look up at him in horror and embarrassment rises from my chest, up my neck to burn my face. I am hot and cold at the same time. "Did you do this?"

"You mean, did I change your clothes?" he asks with a nonchalant air.

"Yes," I say, hating that the word comes out breathless. "Did you see me *naked*?" I cross my arms over my chest, feeling self-conscious at the turn in the conversation.

"I have seen countless women naked in my lifetime," he says. It's answer enough for me.

I can't think with him this close. I'm embarrassed... infuriated that he's seen me undressed. But most of all, I hate that having him hold me close makes me want him more than I want to end him.

My heartbeat speeds up and I wonder if he can hear it. The way he touches me—holds me—is so familiar it is as if he's been doing it our entire lives.

It makes me feel like a traitor to who I am and to Xander. But even Xander has never made me feel the way Alaric does with just a look.

Clenching my jaw, I use that to fuel my purpose tonight.

I place my hands against his chest, still holding onto the dagger, and push away. His hold gives without resistance.

His mouth ticks up in the corner of one side. "My dear Clara, you flatter me." His arrogant mask slips, and he adds, "No, it was not I who dressed you..."

It takes me a moment to understand what he said.

"I would not force myself on you. I'm not…" He halts on his next words, and I know what they will be before he speaks. His eyes grow wide, and I feel mine react the same. Instead of finishing that thought, he says, "What kind of man do you take me for?"

"You are not a man," I bite out, trying to remain unaffected by him. Inside I shiver, something clenching in my stomach. My body betrays me, wanting what it should fear, the damnable thing that it is.

His nostrils flare as he steps closer. His eyes narrow, a wicked grin forming on his lips. "Make no mistake about this, Clara. I might be a vampire, but I am still a man." Red rings his irises, a mixture of fire and ice.

Suddenly my mouth is dry, and my tongue feels thick and heavy.

"What do you want from me?" I ask.

"Isn't that obvious?"

My life. He wants my life in exchange for the vampire I killed.

"You're insufferable," he says when I don't reply.

"And you're a demon's ass."

"And you should be more careful with that sharp tongue of yours." He leans over me, a dark grin forming across his lips.

I swallow. "Are you going to kill me now?"

He looks at me appraisingly, as though he's weighing his options. "I haven't decided yet."

But I think he has.

"If you're going to kill me, why don't you do it already?" My back bumps into a bookshelf. I hadn't even realized either of us had moved.

Alaric braces his hands on either side of my head, caging me between his arms and body. At some point, I'd dropped the dagger and have taken to clutching at his shirt. Again, my body betrays me, gravitating toward him when I should be repulsed.

"Is that what you want, for me to drink from your veins? You want me to hold you in my arms, to feel my mouth on your warm flesh, as your life leaches from your body? And here I thought you despised my very touch. Yet you are practically begging for it." His voice sends shivers along my body, making every inch of my skin pebble.

He leans in ever so slowly, as though he will do every last thing he spoke of. His canines grow longer as if to emphasize his point.

Despite how I try to be brave when facing him, despite how I tell him that I will never fear him—I know it's a lie. I am afraid of him, afraid of the death he could deliver. Because as many times as I tell myself that my death means Kitty won't have to pay for my actions—I still want to live.

"No, don't." I step to the side, ducking under his arm.

"I didn't think so," he says thoughtfully. "But I would be happy to change that, just say the word."

Outside the wind picks up, howling— or perhaps it's the demons that inhabit the forest surrounding his home. The rain pelts harder against the glass panes, and a roar of thunder cuts through the space between us, rattling the books.

"You're horrible," I say, barely above a whisper, trying to contain my heart that has jumped into my throat. I stare straight ahead at the storm raging outside, the chill of it seeping into this room.

He grips my chin gently between two fingers, turning my face up to look him in the eye.

"Of course," he says in an infuriatingly cool and unaffected voice. "You only see me as the monster that has haunted your nightmares since you were a child. So why should I be anything more?" His thumb traces along my bottom lip. "But the truth is, I am not nearly so monstrous as you."

I slap his hand away and grit my teeth. He can use that silver tongue of his all he likes to spin lies and tell half-truths, but I know it was a vampire that took my mother from me. Damn the laws the vampires have set down for us, I refuse to let a human life mean less than the death of one of theirs.

His hand still cups my cheek, his thumb's movements have stilled, resting on the side of my mouth. I jerk away from him, putting space between us. Every time I put distance between us, one or both of us closes it.

"Don't ever touch me again." Even as I say the words, I wonder how much I mean them.

"As you wish, my dear Clara, but know this—when I touch you again, it will be because you initiate it," he says, emphasizing the first word as if there is no other possibility. "And I will look forward to that day because it will be more than you bargained for."

"You have to know that I would never initiate it." I look sideways at him. He is up to something... and a small, dark part of my soul is intrigued.

His face brightens at that. Crimson rings those dark eyes and a dangerous, sexy smile forms on his mouth. I know whatever happens next will not end well for me.

"Would you like to make a wager?"

"No, I don't," I say without a second's hesitation.

He nods as though he'd somehow known my aversions to such things and absentmindedly forgot. "How about something else, then... a bargain?"

"No, it is the same thing with a different name," I murmur. What is he up to? He runs boiling hot and freezing cold from one minute to the next, and now I can't decipher which it is. "And I don't trust you."

"Come," he says, holding out his hand to me. "We can hardly go on as we are. I will lay out the terms, and then you can decide if you wish to decline or not."

I look at his hand, doubtful. "You won't hold me to it if I hear what you have to say and decide against it?"

"That is correct."

I nod but don't take his hand. He had sworn not to touch me, and I will hold him to it. Alaric's fingers curl into his hand, forming a loose fist that hovers before he drops his arm back to his side. He chuckles lightly at the gesture.

"Pick up the dagger," he says.

My heart stops for a second. There are a thousand different possibilities for him saying that. A fight to the death now, another threat... still, I do as he says, not taking my eyes off him as I do so.

"May I?" he asks, holding out his hand.

I debate whether or not to hand it over. *Did this asshole just make me pick it up when he was capable?* I glare but hand it to him, hilt first.

"That dagger is made of pure night-forged silver." Alaric turns it over in his hand. "It is one of a kind."

His eyes grow distant as he examines the blade as if it were more than what I see in it.

"What does that mean?" I ask softly.

His eyes slowly come back into focus. "It means," he says, clearing his throat. "That it is the strongest metal ever made, and one of the few things that can kill a vampire or a demon. We can heal from *most* injuries, but when cut with night-forged silver, we heal at a human rate, thus when dealt a mortal wound with such a weapon, we will die as a human would."

I swallow thickly. "Why would you tell me that?"

It's common knowledge that vampires cannot survive decapitation or a pierced heart. But however grateful I am for this new information, I wonder why he would reveal such a secret to me, knowing I wish for his death, and why he would ever let me have it in my possession. Unless he is lying, and this is a test.

It's hard to say.

Instead of answering, Alaric extends the dagger's hilt toward me.

I hesitate, then slowly lift my hand and take it, half surprised when he doesn't resist. There's no trick, nothing. He only lowers his arm to his side.

"The bargain I propose is this: if you can manage to draw even a single drop of blood from me with this dagger, then you are free to return home to your family, and I will consider your debt paid in full."

He will let me leave—I can go back to Kitty. My heart stutters in my chest. All I have to do is cut him. Then I swallow the thick lump in my throat that has formed.

"I cut you... and you will let me leave—" I narrow my eyes. "Just like that?"

"Yes."

"What if I kill you?"

He raises his brows. "I would rather you didn't. Drawing a single drop of blood will suffice, and then we can both go back to our lives. I will make sure no vampire comes after you or your sister."

I finally look up to meet his eyes. "What does this have to do with..." I can't bring myself to finish the question.

"Ah, yes," he says as though it's an afterthought. "For every failed attempt, you, my dear Clara, owe me a single kiss."

"What?" I ask, entirely dumbfounded. I can't possibly have

heard him correctly. "A kiss? Why a kiss?"

He prowls forward until we are nearly touching again, but he doesn't go any farther than that. "Because I want to see how sweet that sharp tongue of yours tastes. And because I want you to mean it when you try to stab me through the heart with my own weapon."

Demons and saints... the things those words do to me right now.

"If I agree to this, then you can't compel me ever again. I don't like what it does to me."

"I will accept that term... anything else?"

I shake my head. "I agree to your bargain."

"Good, then it is done."

My veins pulse in anticipation. My tongue darts out to wet my lips, his eyes following the movement. "What will happen if I never try to cut you?"

Alaric shrugs then moves back. "Then, you will stay here until the day you die, and you will never gain your freedom."

CHAPTER
SEVENTEEN
CLARA

Sweat beads along my forehead and drips down the side of my face. Autumn has come in full force and is already being pushed aside for the colder months.

I throw the dagger embedding it in the trunk of the tree I'm using for practice. Chunks of bark are missing from the weeks I've spent trying to perfect my aim, or rather develop it. I would be much better if I had my bow and arrow instead, or someone to teach me how to properly wield a dagger.

Instead, I must figure this out through my own trial and error. Constantly creating bad habits only to realize once I've ingrained them, it is ineffective.

Alaric and I see each other at dinner each night. He doesn't touch me, as per our agreement, nor does he get close.

It's good. Better that he doesn't. When he's near, I forget Xander... his power is too consuming.

I can't be sure he won't try something to get me to unwittingly make contact with him. I swallow down the feeling that is too close to disappointment for my taste.

Gripping the hilt, I brace my other hand against the tree and pull. It doesn't give at first, then like a hot knife through butter, it gives way, and I stumble back several steps. The strike was good but off target.

I wipe my forehead with the back of my hand then rest my back against the tree. I'm more comfortable with the blade in my hand, it feels more like an extension of me.

I turn my head to look up at the window on the third floor of the manor. I see the faint light of a fire roaring in Alaric's study. I can't tell if he's in there or not.

With every passing day, I grow more and more restless, anxious to get home to my sister. I hope she is doing well. I have sent two letters but have yet to hear back, which makes me worry all the more.

I have asked her about Xander as my letters to him have also gone unanswered. It makes me wonder if they are getting to him at all. He would have been worried when I never showed up that night as we had planned.

It is only the prospect of me attempting to cut Alaric and

failing... the thought of his mouth on mine that I cannot risk. It seems a simple enough request, but I can't help but feel as though it will lead to something far more dangerous than a simple kiss would imply.

I need to draw blood from him soon... but worry is making me hesitate.

I move around the tree, using it to hide my body as I slip the sheathed blade into my pocket and practice ways of reaching for it that seem natural. I do everything I can think of with the dagger, wanting every movement with it to feel as natural as everything else, so when I do go to strike, Alaric will not see it coming.

One glance at the sky is enough to tell me that it is nearly time for dinner. I will go to my room and change, then the two of us will dine with soft music playing on the phonograph in the background, and then he will ask me the same question he does every night.

I arrive before him. It has become more and more common. Every night thus far, I have come to dinner telling myself that tonight will be the night I will draw blood... but every night, the thought of his kiss has me halting my plans.

I take my seat and wait. A warm fire blazes in the hearth, snapping and crackling. I take a sip of wine to temper my nerves. As I set the crystal glass down, music drifts into the room.

Then he appears in the doorway. Immediately my stomach clenches. And it is because of that reaction to seeing him walk into the same room that I have stayed my hand.

As of late, he has shown me less and less of the telltale signs of vampirism. I think he does it to play with my mind, to lull me into feeling safe around him. But I cannot let my guard down, no matter how human he might appear.

"Good evening, Clara," he says, taking his seat. "Have you been waiting long?"

He looks tired tonight.

"I've only just sat down myself."

Our conversation is stiff and scripted. But every night we continue this charade, it grows harder and harder to remember that this man is not my friend. We would both like to see the other dead.

We eat in silence. I notice he barely touches his food. Eventually, he sets his fork and knife down and looks to me for the first time since entering.

"I will retire to my study now if you'll excuse me."

I dip my chin in a single nod.

He seems paler than usual, dark shadows have formed under his eyes. Alaric stands then asks the same question he does before we part ways. "Will you be attempting to draw blood tonight?"

"No," I say automatically.

I'm unsure if he expects me to ever answer yes, or if he expects a no and an attempt.

He nods once, and then he walks from the room.

I look down at my plate of food, barely touched. It is as delicious as everything else I've eaten since being here, but something about tonight's dinner has left me unsettled, and I have lost my appetite.

I am not worried about him. I'm not. I can't be.

Pushing away from the table, I stand and walk out. I make my way down the hall faster than usual. I am almost running by the time I stop at the landing that leads to the third floor. I grip the banister tightly.

What am I doing?

I take a step away. I will not check on him tonight.

I keep moving down the hall and enter my room, closing the door securely behind me.

There is something strange about tonight... something different than every other night. I pace, nearly crawling out of my skin with anticipation.

I busy myself, trying to read by the fire as I do every night after dinner, but I find I can't focus on a single word on the page. After reading the same paragraph a dozen times over, I close the book and set it aside. I itch with the need to do something, but I can't decide on what.

Every dress in my armoire has at least one hidden pocket sewn into it. I have practiced for hours with the dagger, and yet I can think of nothing else.

I pace the length of my room. Deftly, my hand reaches for the dagger and pulls it. Over and over. Yet it seems with every other step, my thoughts return to the vampire and to the disappointment I felt when he left dinner early... to the way he looked, sallow, and unlike himself.

"No," I chide aloud. *I don't care about him. I can't.*

Stopping in the middle of the room, I return the dagger to my pocket and stare down into the palms of my hands, as if they might literally hold the answer to the question I've yet to ask. A question I can barely think and will not speak.

I go to the bedside table and pick up my worn and tattered novel close to falling apart.

"Oh, Kitty... what should I do?" I whisper.

How can I want to return to her and yet refuse to do what I must here first?

Because I am afraid. Afraid of failing because that would mean facing something I don't know if I'll ever be ready for.

What is wrong with me that I am concerned for a *vampire*, of all things, because he looks unwell?

Like a bolt of lightning, it strikes me why tonight is different than all our previous ones.

It's not worry for him that made me nervous—it was the realization that he is off, weak, tired, slow, something, and I would be a fool not to take advantage of it. I know killing him would be the best, but I wonder if I am brave enough to follow through anymore. But I will settle for drawing blood and winning my freedom.

If there ever was a time to try, it is now. Because I must return to my sister as soon as possible, to Xander and start my life, and to get away from the vampire before I fall for this illusion of humanity more than I already have.

I pat the dagger hidden at my side and then head out of my room and into the halls and up the stairs to Alaric's personal study.

CHAPTER
EIGHTEEN
ALARIC

Satiated. Not completely... but enough. I recline in my chair at my desk and gaze into the fire across from me. I have nearly forgotten how completely satisfying it is to give in to what I am. Though I frown. Were it not for Cherno, when I drank that willing girl's blood after dinner, I would have been far too close to losing control.

I was careless, and the girl could have died. I had overestimated my willpower, and the moment my fangs had pierced her skin, she was nearly lost. Rosalie would have had my head for my carelessness of a donor.

"You almost waited too long," Cherno says from their perch on my shoulder.

"I know."

"You put that girl and Clara's life at risk." There's more than a touch of admonishment in their voice.

"No, I wouldn't—"

Cherno flaps their wings, smacking me on the side of my head. "You would. You can only control your bloodlust for so long until it takes over on its own. Do not be a fool, Alaric."

I clench my jaw and reach up, scooping them off my shoulder and looking into those big red eyes. "Stop that, you little demon." I drop my head. "I don't know... I haven't wanted to," I admit. "I can't even take a sip at dinner without Clara glaring at me."

"Then bite her and take her blood."

I shake my head.

They hop down from my hand and crawl over the desk. "What do you hope to gain from this bargain?"

Again, I shake my head. "I should hate her... I *do* hate her for what she did to Rosalie... but every time she is near—"

I want her.

It is a damning truth. A curse to want the very creature who took away the one soul I had left in this world.

"Leave me. I have other business more important than some damned bargain with a mortal," I say, resting my face in my hands.

Cherno says nothing more. There is only the flapping of their small leather wings, and then I am alone with the crackling fire.

I look at the opened letter on my desk. I had assumed Elizabeth was once again requesting my presence, but the news was far worse. It had, in part, been one of the reasons I'd made the deal with Clara... that coupled with my own selfish reasons. There was little more I could have done, except demand she allow me to mark her, to bind her to me—but she would have refused outright. I would have wanted her to refuse.

After a long moment, I stand. *Enough moping. Enough dwelling.* There is nothing I can do to stop the future from happening. Snatching the crystal decanter from the shelf, I pour some of the amber liquid into one of the glasses. I throw my head back and relish in the burn of it. Then I pour another, sipping this one slowly, enjoying the taste.

I freeze as I turn. Clara stands in the doorway, ready for a fight. But my mind is too weary for such a thing tonight.

"Good evening," I say. "Are you here to draw blood?"

She marches up to me, a storm in her deep brown eyes, the color nearly drowned out by her pupils.

"I... I would rather *die* than kiss you," Clara hisses.

I nod and turn away, taking another draw from my glass. It has been less than an hour since I have consumed the blood of a mortal woman, and still the urge to pull Clara to me is strong.

I rest an arm on the fireplace mantle and get lost in my thoughts, hoping she will leave if I ignore her.

Seconds later, I realize that small hope is in vain when she moves to stand before me, hands on her hips. I take another sip, her eyes following the movement, and I see the moment she realizes it isn't blood.

"What is that?" she asks.

"Brandy," I say. Then after a short pause, I add, "Would you like some?"

She eyes the liquid suspiciously. Her gaze roams to the decanter behind me on the shelf, then slowly, she nods. Good. The last thing I want to do with her right now is fight.

I pour her a decent amount, and she is achingly careful to take it by the bottom of the glass to avoid touching me. A move I find both amusing and disappointing.

Clara sits on the floor with her back up against the desk, foregoing the chair before the fireplace, or the one behind the desk. She is an odd human. I have seen more than my fair share of ladies, and Clara is nothing like them. Were her qualities to be written down and applied to anyone else, they would seem undesirable, but she has a way of being comfortable in her own skin in such a way that those same qualities fit her like a glove.

I grab the decanter and sit on the floor next to her. I watch every movement as she brings the glass to her lips and takes a sip. She sighs and leans back, so her spine is relaxed rather than ramrod straight for once.

"This is good... thank you."

Clara holds the glass in her lap. The fire and storm in her when she first entered the room has fizzled out.

The hour ticks by in silence, then two, and then three. As we each empty our glasses, I refill them until every last drop from the decanter is gone. It is strange to sit next to someone I should have killed the moment I discovered her crime, knowing she wishes for my death as well—and have a moment of quiet and... I wouldn't call it understanding, but something akin to it.

The small clock on the mantle chimes three in the morning.

She turns to me, setting her empty glass on top of the desk. "I should go."

I want to protest. I want to ask her to stay until the sun rises. Instead, I nod and rise with her.

Her hand goes to her side, pressing against her skirt. I know instantly from her tell that she has the dagger stashed away there. Then she drops her chin and says, "Thank you." The tone is demure and overly sweet and false.

Clara pulls back her arm and thrusts it forward. I catch her wrist easily enough. She's too slow, even if she hadn't had alcohol dimming her senses. I keep my hand where it is, even when the strength goes out of her arm, and the dagger clatters to the floor.

"That didn't take long for you to change your mind."

Her eyes are locked on my hand, encircling her small wrist. My grip is light, and she could pull away if she tried. But she doesn't move.

"Now, it's time to pay for your failure."

Now, she drags her gaze to my face. I watch her throat bob as she swallows nervously. Pink stains her cheeks, but there's heat in her eyes—fury. "I want to renegotiate the deal."

"A deal is a deal," I say, setting my glass next to hers. I lean forward and turn my face slightly, pointing to my cheek.

Clara lets out a slow breath then leans forward, her eyes close

150

as her mouth nears my jaw. I turn and her lips are on mine. I pull her close with one arm and tangle the fingers of my other hand into her hair.

Her lips are softer than I imagined, and for a brief second, her mouth is hard and unyielding, but then she becomes pliant against me, responding to every movement and demand I make. The brandy is sweeter on her lips.

I could get lost in her.

Clara's teeth graze the bottom of my lip, then clamp down.

She lets out a soft gasp of surprise as I pull away. The slightest taste of copper is on the tip of my tongue. She bit me and broke the skin. It is a curious thing for a human to bite a vampire. Heat builds in my core, along with amusement.

I throw my head back and laugh. I think I will enjoy this one.

Clara presses her palms to my chest and pushes herself from my arms.

"You cheated," she accuses.

I shake my head, not regretting anything. "No, my dear Clara, you were the one who tried to cheat your way out of our bargain. I told you that when you try to cut me, I want you to mean it. If you didn't want the kiss, then you shouldn't have made such a poor attempt."

Anger colors her face now as she glares. Her fists clench at her sides.

"The attempt was sloppy. You rushed it," I say.

I wonder if she will insist that the no touching rule will remain in effect when she isn't trying to stab me. But she doesn't, and that pleases me more than it should.

She sputters but, in the end, says nothing.

"If you want to have any chance at drawing blood from a vampire, you need to work on your tells," I say, bending down to pick up the fallen dagger. I hand it to her by taking her hand and pressing the hilt into her palm, emphasizing the point that she initiated the touching. "Not to mention, your timing and speed could not be worse. You will need to do far more than expertly hide this on your person—which I will assume is always on you."

Clara is shaking with indignation, she huffs and spins on her heel, storming out of the room.

I can practically taste her anger in the air.

She can detest me all she likes, but she will thank me someday.

CHAPTER
NINETEEN
CLARA

His kiss is seared on my lips and upon my very soul. It lingers long after I fall asleep. I press my fingers to my mouth, and my eyes slide shut as a shiver runs over my body.

Rolling to my side, I stare unseeing at my surroundings as the watery light of the day washes over everything. I came to my room to nap after breakfast and have been here ever since. But like most nights lately, I haven't been able to fall asleep for all the noise of my unending thoughts swirling through my head.

My attempts to draw even the smallest drop of blood from him inevitably end in failure and a kiss. It feels as though it has become a sick game between us—one where I seek him out for these moments.

"Miss Valmont," Mr. Steward's voice drifts through the door as he knocks twice. For a second, I lay still, thinking about pretending to be asleep. Then he speaks again. "A letter has come for you in the post this afternoon."

My heart is in my throat in an instant. I fling off the blankets and leap off the bed. Throwing open the armoire, I grab the first dress I can and pull it on, not bothering to button the back. I hurry to the door and fling it open, coming face to face with the butler, who stares at me with wide eyes.

"A letter?" I ask breathlessly.

The butler lifts his eyebrows at my excitement, then, entirely too calm, he says, "Yes, Miss."

I have been waiting for a response since the day I wrote my first letter to Kitty. It's all I can do to stop myself from reaching out and snatching the letter out of his grasp. He seems to be moving in slow motion.

The man has never shown an ounce of emotion one way or the other. I wonder if he is even capable of them.

"Thank you," I say once I have the letter in my grasp. My hands tremble.

"You weren't at lunch, Miss. Do you wish for me to bring you something to eat?"

I am a little hungry, but offering to bring me something seems to leave a bitter taste in his mouth, so I shake my head. "No, thank you."

"Very well," Mr. Steward says, bowing slightly before walking away.

I close the door with my foot and lean back against it. It takes me two tries to open the letter. Eventually, I break the seal and open it. It's a single page with a few short paragraphs.

Dear Clara,

I was relieved to get your letters, having feared you would have been killed by that horrid monster that first night. All of your letters have put me in the best of spirits, and I would like to think that on those days my health has improved even if just a little. I will admit I put off answering your first letters in the hope that you would have returned before a response would have reached you.

I am glad to hear you are alive and well. I miss you more than words can say.

Hurry, sweet sister, and dispose of that monster so that you may return home to me where you are needed.

Your loving sister,

Kathrine

I flip the page over but there is nothing more. I can't help the ache of disappointment that she didn't write more, that she didn't even speak a word of Xander, or if he ever received my letters to him or if he hasn't received them—if he knows why I left. Surely, he knows I have every intention of returning.

I wonder if Mr. Devereaux is sending my letters or having them destroyed... it would explain why Xander hasn't written back, but then why did Kitty not mention him?

I rub my temples with my fingers. There is no way I am going to know for sure. I must keep trying to win my freedom.

Folding the letter, I shove it into my pocket and sink down to the floor. An awful feeling gnaws at the back of my mind. As much as I want to return to my life, to those I love, there have been times where I have become consumed with life here. I press my fingers to my mouth, pull in a deep breath, and hold it. My cheeks burn at the thought of every kiss that has happened between the vampire and me.

I have tried over a dozen times to draw blood, and each failure has been a betrayal to Xander. No matter how many times I tell myself it is necessary for me to eventually leave here, I know a part of me wants it. Every kiss is different, some are cold and quick... and with others, I nearly lose my senses. But every single one has erased the memory of Xander's kisses, bit by bit. I am afraid that one day soon, I will not be able to recall a single kiss or the feel of his embrace any longer.

Alaric might not be compelling me, but I wonder if he uses some demonic power whenever he is close. I don't see how there could be any other explanation for it.

Nothing I have done thus far has worked. I need to change my strategy. While I want nothing more than to rid the world of vampires and avenge everyone who has ever been taken or murdered by one… I do not need to kill Alaric as I have been attempting. I only need to draw a single drop of blood to earn my freedom.

I don't need the strength or speed to pierce a heart, only a small flick of my wrist. A scratch.

It will be enough to just be free and return home.

Standing, I stretch before reaching behind me to fasten up the back of the dress. I grab the dagger from the night table and head out of my rooms.

I stop first at the library, but there is no one there and the fire in the hearth is dying down. I swallow my nerves, squaring my shoulders, and head up the staircase to the third floor. Since that first night we drank on the floor of his study, he has not even tried to enforce the ban he'd set—so I'm not sure why I'm so nervous about going up there now.

I bypass the first two rooms and head straight for the last door.

When I peek in, I see the fire is roaring, Alaric's jacket is slung over the back of the large wing-backed chair near the fireplace, and an open book sits, spine up, on the cushion.

He's been reading, and by the looks of things, he will return shortly. I pick up the book and turn it over, glancing at the title before opening it up to the beginning.

"Will you be joining the master for tea," the butler asks from the doorway. "Or are you snooping through his things?"

I snap the book shut, having nearly jumped out of my skin at being caught. Mr. Steward holds a tray with a single china cup and a teapot.

"There is a personal matter I wish to discuss with him," I say with a bite to my words.

He grunts and nods once, setting the tray on the desk, then pouring a cup and placing it on the small round table next to the chair. He leaves without another word or glance in my direction.

I breathe out once he's gone. Looking at the steeping tea, I know Alaric will be back soon enough. I reach inside my pocket and pull out the dagger, positioning it under the book in my hand. It takes a few attempts to find something comfortable and natural enough to hold the blade while I appear to be reading.

I stand in place, flipping through the pages as though I'm reading. But all of my attention is on the sounds around me. Listening for him to return and catch him by surprise with a scratch of the blade.

My shoulders grow stiff, and the tea has cooled. I shift in place, growing uncomfortable.

I huff to myself. Who asks for tea and then doesn't return in time to drink it before it gets cold? It feels like I have been waiting on him for hours at this point, and I am already a good portion through the book. I'm in danger of finishing it before he gets back.

"You didn't even smile at that part," Alaric's silky voice whispers in my ear.

I spin, trying not to drop the book as I swipe at him.

Once again, Alaric has managed to stop me with one hand

staying my wrist only by his preternatural strength. He takes the book from me and closes it, then drops it on the chair. He moves my arm to the side, stepping into me until we are only a breath apart.

I swallow thickly as he stares down at me. His dark blue eyes are ringed with red. I should be afraid, but I don't think he will bite. Not once in all the time we've spent together has he once tried to bite me.

He takes my chin in his free hand and then his mouth crashes down on mine. His hand moves around to the back of my head, keeping me locked in place. The kiss is hard, and I swear my already swollen lips will bruise. Anger sparks through me and I growl in frustration.

His movements still for a second, but he doesn't pull away, but now there's a hunger in his kiss, a desperation I've never known before, and it's dragging me under... consuming me.

His tongue grazes my lip, and I part willingly. I can't get close enough to him. He tastes like brandy and something sweet. My fingers grip at the back of his shirt, and I try to pull him closer... closer... heat builds in my veins.

The world slowly slips away, and there is only him and me, and this moment.

When my fingers find their way to the buttons of his shirt, his movements slow. His hands snake down my arms until he's gripping my wrists, and halting my actions.

Then slowly, as if coming up for air, we part as if we were magnets drawn to each other but are being pulled apart by some outside force.

Alaric backs up a step then reaches around me, picking up the book. His tongue darts across his bottom lip in a quick movement, drawing my attention to his mouth once more. For a second, I wonder if he'll kiss me again, but as time ticks by, he doesn't.

"Goodnight, dear Clara," he says gently. He dips his chin, then turns and leaves me alone in his study.

I sink down to the floor, my weak knees no longer wanting to support my weight, and bite down hard on my bottom lip.

When I finally manage to slow my racing heart, I reach into my pocket and pull out Kitty's letter, thinking of home, and of Xander. His kisses were sweet but wholly unremarkable in comparison to Alaric's.

I should feel horrified, but I don't.

Closing my eyes, I take three deep breaths before opening them again. A real kiss can't have this effect. I am more convinced than ever now that Alaric is using his powers over me. Not compelling me, but something in a similar vein.

I am left feeling like I might be in trouble, far worse than I initially thought.

CHAPTER
TWENTY
CLARA

Pathetic. For the past three days I have been claiming to be ill, to avoid Alaric.

The sky is gray from horizon to horizon. The rain coming and going at regular intervals until it's impossible to tell what time of day it is without finding a clock. Of which there are exactly zero in this room.

The only way I've been able to know the time is when Mrs. Westfield or Elise stopped by with meals.

I am going stir crazy confined to this small place. It is beginning to feel a lot like a beautifully decorated prison cell of my own making.

Small… it's absurd to consider my room to be small. But back home, I would never stay inside for long.

I pause in my pacing before the window and stare unseeing out the window at the gray, cloud covered sky. I press my fingertips to my mouth.

Demons and saints...

I remember the moment the kiss went from hard and punishing to something much different. It had lasted longer than any of the previous times, and by the time one or both of us pulled away, he could have asked for anything in this world, I would have said yes.

And that scares me to death.

This must end. I know it must, even though my gut twists at the thought. And it is because of that that I know I will not be able to withstand the hold he has on me for much longer.

Finally, having grown too restless to stay hidden any longer, I head into the bathing room to wash up.

Once I am finished dressing, I make my way downstairs. The table in the dining room is set, but only for one person.

Lydia is finishing up arranging the various china and items. I catch the scent of the food that normally triggers my appetite and find that, today, I have none.

She lifts her head and takes me in, but rather than saying anything she turns and heads back into the kitchen. I sit in the usual spot and pour myself a cup of tea. I sip on it slowly, hoping it will ease my stomach. I hate to let the food go to waste after so many years of never having enough, but the thought of eating right now is unappealing.

I push away from the table and stand just as Elise comes through the door.

"I saw you," she says, her words accusing.

Gone is the timid girl who asked if she could speak frankly.

"What are you talking about?"

Her golden eyebrows furrow in anger as she steps further into the room. "I saw you try to stab him the other night."

My throat tightens. I'm not sure what to say to that. This whole time I had assumed that none of the staff was aware of how Alaric and I interact.

Elise looks hurt as if I personally assaulted her. I don't know why, but I don't wish to share the details of my bargain with Alaric to her or anyone else.

"That matter doesn't concern you," I say, then I stride away.

The manor is quite possibly the largest structure I have ever set foot in, and yet today it feels confining. Having no desire to spend any more time in my rooms, I wander the halls until I end up at the foot of the stairs that lead to the third floor.

My usual tactics have not worked to win my freedom. I need to rethink my strategy. I have no idea where to begin, and for this moment, I am too weary to practice or come up with a new plan.

The library seems to call to me now. I have been here for several weeks and have been too preoccupied to spend any significant amount of time there. I could do with a little mental stimulation after the boredom I put myself through.

A fire burns hot in the hearth, chasing away the chill that was present the last time I was here.

I run my hands across the spines humming a tune Mother used to sing to us when we were little as I look for a title or three that catch my eye.

"Are you tone-deaf, or is this a new kind of torture you intend to inflict upon me until I send you away?" Alaric asks.

I whirl around, and Alaric is right behind me. My hand flies to my chest as my heart attempts to leap out of my skin. "Demons and saints, you startled me. It's a nasty habit you've picked up."

Instinct has me reaching for the dagger I always keep at my side. Alaric's eyes glint with mirth, and that is enough to still my hand. When I don't immediately try to stab him, one of his brows raises in question.

"Are you missing something?" he asks, a single dark brow arches.

"No," I say. I have so many thoughts whirling around in my mind I can't decide which of them to say. *I am too tired to play this game, or I am afraid of what one more failure will do to me,* or a million other confessions. So, I say nothing.

His eyes darken as if he can sense all of this and more.

"Then I will leave you to it," he says, and with a half bow, he turns to leave.

I blink, fully expecting him to flirt or find some reason to touch me. I've grown so used to it that the absence of his touch feels strange.

"Clara," he says, stopping in the doorway, not quite looking in my direction. "If something is ailing you, I expect you to speak up." And then he's gone.

I'm not sure what that was about. He couldn't possibly be worried about me... could he? I told Mrs. Westfield that I was sick, so perhaps she told him.

I already have enough things to mull over to last me a lifetime without adding to it.

I continue my search for a book and eventually settle on a thick tome of fairytales. I settle into the window seat at the back of the library and open the book. The leather binding groans for being used for what I assume must be the first time.

And then I get lost in new worlds I have never begun to imagine.

Blinking open my eyes, I find that the gray has cleared and the remains of the sun's rays are sinking below the horizon. I stretch and close the book, having fallen asleep at some point.

It's dark now, which means the servants have all left for the day. *I wonder where they go... home to their families?* There must be a small town nearby, within a short walking or riding distance.

I push the blanket off my legs. One of the servants must have placed it on me when they came to fetch me for lunch or dinner.

I find I have an appetite for food, but since the sun has set, the staff is gone, and I don't want to help myself to whatever is in the kitchen. It feels a bit forward to go into their space and rummage around.

Being listless is unusual. But I find myself missing Kitty more and more as of late, made worse by the fact that I could see her soon if I only possessed the skill to do what was needed.

At this rate, I will never earn my freedom.

I close the door behind me and lean against it.

My vision blurs. I tilt my head back, trying to blink away the emotions that have welled up unexpectedly. A hot tear escapes and runs down my cheek. I roughly wipe it away with the back of my hand.

I reach back and struggle with the buttons of my dress until it's undone and let it slide to the floor, then walk to where my nightdress is laid out for me over the foot of the bed and slide it over my head. The material reminds me of the white sacrifice like dresses the devoted wear for their vampires.

I finger the thin material. It's strange. Something like this should make me feel like one of them... but I don't.

I do not see vampires as gods as the devoted do, and I certainly don't see Alaric that way. Though I don't see him as just a vampire anymore.

I might be a vampire, but I am still a man.

He is more human than I expected. True, what I had expected, was for him to kill me or turn me into a mindless slave right away, and weeks later, I am still myself.

Bleary-eyed and tired, I crawl into bed, ready to sleep. I am determined to resume training tomorrow.

I pull the blanket up over me and snuggle into my pillow.

Sharp pain lances through my hand and down my arm. Bolting upright, I withdraw my arm from under the pillow and stare down at the long gash running from the middle of my hand down the side of my arm. Red... so much red. Blood wells up, trailing along my skin and drips onto the sheets.

I'm lightheaded as shock courses through me. With my uninjured hand, I lift the pillow and toss it away. Laying there, the edge lined with my blood is a shard of glass. I lift it, it's not terribly large, but the damage could have been much worse.

A violent shiver runs through me. I look back to my cut—blood drips on my sheets.

I need to stop the bleeding.

I walk to the bathroom, the blood leaving a morbid trail. It seems to be bleeding faster now. Inside the bathroom, I pause to look around for something to use as a bandage. The servants must have forgotten to replace the towels earlier.

My legs feel week and cold envelops my entire body. *I just want to sit for a minute and think.*

I look from the slice in my hand to the shard I hold in the other, unsure what to do.

The door to the room swings open, hitting the wall with a hard crack.

Alaric stands in the doorway, eyes blazing, the red ring is nearly glowing in the dim light, his fangs have extended, and there is anger in his expression. His chest heaves with labored breaths.

This is bad. This is very, very bad.

"I'm cut," I say stupidly. Of course, he can see that. I drop the shard of glass. It cracks as it hits the white tile.

He looks less human at this moment than I have ever seen him before. I think now might be the moment he finally kills me — bargain or no bargain.

"Clara, what have you done?" he demands, crouching before me.

I flinch, expecting him to lose himself at the sight and smell of blood, but he doesn't.

"I don't..." I look from him back to my hand. There is so much blood on the floor. I don't think it's right. "I went to bed, and there was glass..."

Alaric's hands tightly grip my shoulders, almost painfully. "I will not let you take the easy way out of our agreements. If you die, then it will be by my hand and my hand alone."

He grips my elbow and pulls my injured arm forward to examine it, and I swear that the red in his eye threatens to swallow up every last bit of blue. Then without warning, he grips the hem of my nightgown and rips. I gasp at the violence of the motion, but his hands move deftly, wrapping the strip of cloth to stanch the bleeding.

I shake my head. Does he think I did this on purpose? My tongue darts out between my lips as I try to form words to explain what happened, but he picks up the piece of glass and stands before I get a chance to and says, "Do not move."

Then he leaves the room. I have to blink several times. My eyes are playing tricks on me because there is no way anyone can move that fast.

I hold my breath for a long moment, watching the blood seep through the white, darkening it, spreading... spreading... spreading. When my lungs ache, I release my breath.

"Clara," he says my name, kneeling before me and setting a small black doctor's bag at his side. I scoot back, but he grabs hold of me, keeping me from retreating. "Be still," he orders.

He releases my arm only to lift my hand to unwrap the makeshift bandage. Alaric's fingers caress my wrist. I want to jerk away. He is helping me, but it feels too intimate.

Instead, I turn my head and gaze at a small spot on the tile while he works. There's pressure and the occasional sting as he takes care of it.

While he works, he mumbles something about it not being too deep. Already it feels better, but I can't tell him that.

His fingers are still for a moment, and when he doesn't continue, I look at my hand, wrapped from palm to the middle of my arm, holding my hand with both of his, staring at it.

"Thank you," I say when he still doesn't move or speak.

He looks at me, and I tug on my hand. Reluctantly, he releases me, only to lean forward until he hovers over me. My gaze flicks to his mouth, and I think he might kiss me until I see the look in his eyes—dark, and distant, and not a single spot of red.

He picks me up and carries me into the main room, setting me on a chair while he changes the sheets, then lays me on the bed. Once more, he hovers, his gaze focused on my injury.

"Am I so terrible to be around that you would prefer this?" he asks.

My mind is still fuzzy.

"I—" I start then cut off, not sure how to answer.

"You need to sleep more now," he says.

I try to speak again but Alaric straightens his back and pulls a white handkerchief from his pocket, then begins scooping up what is left of a glass vase scattered over the night table. *When had I managed to knock that over?* I must have been far more tired than I realized if I broke it without noticing.I don't even remember seeing it at all.

Then he leaves without so much as another word. The door closes softly behind him, and I am left feeling strange and melancholy.

CHAPTER
TWENTY-ONE
ALARIC

I wish to go to her, but after what she attempted last night, I don't think I can bear to look at her. There is something about what she did last night that haunts me, though I cannot put the feeling to words in an accurate way.

So far, she has not sought me out as usual. Though if she did, I am not sure what I would say.

Pulling back from the woman whose name I don't know, nor care to learn, I wipe away the drop of blood at the corner of my mouth.

"Go, and do not return," I say, infusing power into my voice, compelling her to obey.

She straightens and turns to leave, walking out of the atrium's doors to the carriage waiting to take her back home. Once she has departed, I sit on a stone bench next to the water's raised pool in the middle of the room.

Roses grow all around, their petals beginning to close as the sun continues to lower. The sweet heady perfume of them is almost cloying. The warm light seeps in through all sides of the glass room, making the bronze arches that meet in the center of the domed ceiling glitter like gold.

Cherno flies into the room and hovers before me. "You must mark her."

"She despises my very being to the extent that she would rather die than suffer my presence."

Cherno flutters their wings, flying around me in nonsensical patterns. "Do you wish her to like you?"

"No," I say, perhaps a little too quickly. I want Clara, but that is not the same as wanting her affections. Most importantly, there is the reason I brought her here in the first place. "I want her to pay for what she has done."

A loud squeak fills the air as Cherno swoops and dives. The little beast is laughing.

"I'm glad one of us finds this amusing," I say dryly.

"Strange," they say, landing on the brick ledge of the pool. "You say you want her to pay, but her punishment is a kiss. Are you saying a kiss from you is punishment?"

"Silence, you little demon," I snap. I don't know why I allow this demon the freedom they have. No other vampire would tolerate such obstinance. "She cannot stand me any more than I can stand her. The kiss was never supposed to happen. It was intended to deter her from trying to kill me at all."

"You could always refuse to follow through."

"I could," I say. "But then she'll know the threat isn't real, and I'd have to watch out for her attempts on my life even in my sleep." I shake my head. "No, this is the most effective way."

I rest my forearms on my knees and slump my shoulders, letting my head hang. She was never supposed to try... And now I am more certain than ever I'd be unable to kill her. I should let her go. There is no longer a reason to keep her here, the misery it causes her brings me no joy.

But pride and anger for the loss of Rosalie keeps me from freeing her yet. And I am left not sure what to do with Clara.

Cherno takes to the air and says, "Kill her or mark her, Alaric, you cannot have it any other way. You might have avoided the claiming in the past, but you know how this works."

Then Cherno flies away.

In the quiet, my thoughts grow loud. I scrub my face with my hands. In my attempt to punish a murderess, I have unwittingly set myself up for a punishment of my own.

I make my way through the halls toward the third floor. I need to forget if only for a night.

It isn't until I am rounding the corner to climb the stairs that I hear the softest footfalls. Reaching out, I grab Clara's wrist, preventing her from skewering me with Rosalie's dagger. The point of the blade rests against the material of my vest but does not pierce it.

Her eyes are wide as she looks from my face to where I stopped her. Pride swells on her face that she got closer to drawing blood than ever before.

It twists something inside of me.

Her face is flushed, her breathing a little too fast as if she'd been running through the manor.

"I see your hand has healed up nicely," I say as if we had not spent the past week avoiding each other between the two of us. "I half expected to find you asleep in the library again."

I move her arm and pull her into me. As I lower my mouth to hers she rises up on her toes to meet me. There is nothing hesitant in her this time. Now she leans into it, deepening it as she presses the length of her body against mine.

Fuck. This woman will destroy me if she doesn't learn how to attack a vampire soon.

I pull away and release her as I move to walk around her.

She strikes out, her arm swinging toward me, and I block the strike with little effort. "Come now, Clara, you can do far better than that. It's like you weren't even trying."

Clara narrows her eyes at the accusation. "You know what I think? I think you're regretting this bargain you made with me."

Once more, I pull her to me and kiss her, cupping her face with both hands. She has more than enough time to stab me with the dagger, but instead, she wraps her arms around my neck, pushing up on her toes.

This is not enough. The small distance our clothes create feels like a chasm between us.

May the Otherworld destroy me where I stand—I should kill her for what she did, but right now all I can think about is how I want to feel every inch of her bare skin against mine, and bury myself deep inside her.

Her teeth scrape my lip, reminiscent of the time she bit me. My hands skim down the sides of her body. And then she groans into my mouth, and I want to devour her in every sense of the word... and it's then I know I am about to lose myself to her.

I run one hand along her arm, then take the dagger from her hand in the same instant I step back. With a flick of my wrist, the blade embeds into the wall up to its hilt.

"Enough," I say. Though my body aches to return to her. If I allow this to continue, I don't think either of us will be able to stop at just a kiss.

Like a coward, I leave her standing there as I retreat to my sanctuary.

CHAPTER
TWENTY-TWO
CLARA

He was right when he said I didn't even try with that second attempt. But I am tired. Tired of feeling guilty. And so, so, so tired of always fighting. I want to give in to something else, even with this man who has taken my life... I had wanted so much more than that simple kiss.

With every kiss, I feel as though I fall deeper under his spell. He might not be compelling me, he must be using some power to make me want him as I do.

I got close last night to drawing blood. Less than an inch... but I am nowhere near as skilled as I need to be, and I am afraid that if I wait much longer, I will be truly and utterly lost to him in every way. There is no other explanation for wanting, a creature who ripped my family apart and took me from the man I meant to spend the rest of my life with.

The song of morning birds drifts through my open window. A horse whinnies from out front, drawing me to the window. Mr. Devereaux mounts a large roan steed, pushing it into a run as soon as he's seated and heads south. This could be the chance I've been waiting for.

If I stay here, I will die. I know that now. But if I run and Alaric finds me, he might kill me.

Either way, I am a dead woman. The only difference is when and where. If I must die, then I want it to be on my terms, I want to be free.

And just like that, I breathe a little easier knowing I have decided my own fate.

I hurry across the room and throw open the armoire. Ignoring the section of dresses, I search the drawers. The first is stuffed with an assortment of corsets. *Definitely not what I need.* There are more drawers filled with all kinds of underthings. Also, not what I'm looking for.

Then, in the bottom drawer, there are two bundles of clothing. I reach in and pull one out. A pair of fitted trousers and a shirt. I don't waste a second removing the dress I spent all night huddled up in.

Donning the men's clothes feels more like home, familiar, and what I'm used to. Unlike my own, however, they fit me like a glove. As though someone had gone so far as to take my measurements before creating them.

At some point, Alaric had these made for me. As warmth seeps into my heart, I banish it. I must leave. I cannot be grateful to him now.

I slip the dagger into my boot, making sure it is hidden but still accessible.

I stroll through the manor as if today is just another day where I attempt to entertain myself. It is the perfect time to leave. He won't realize I'm gone until it's too late.

"Good morning, Miss," Mr. Steward's level voice stops me in my tracks as I reach the foyer.

I give him a strained smile. My heart picks up its pace. Not even out of the manor, and I've been caught.

He clearly doesn't approve of my outfit, a fact made clear by the slight curl to his lip. "Will you be wanting breakfast?"

I shake my head. "No, not today."

After a pause, he says, "Very well."

I turn and hurry outside before he can take up more of my time. The man makes me uneasy.

I make my way through the gardens and toward the forest in a wandering line, trying to appear as if I don't have a destination by keeping a leisurely pace, though doing so kills me.

I pause at the tree line, watching the shadows dance and play beneath the canopy. There are still several hours of daylight left.

I should make it out of the forest and to a town before night falls if I hurry.

It will be a long journey.

I look back at the intimidating manor. What will Alaric do when he realizes I'm no longer here?

It doesn't matter… Kitty needs me, and every second I linger is one more that I lose escaping this place.

Maybe together we can take the money I saved, leave, and find a place of our own without Father, somewhere the vampire will never find us.

And Father can learn to pay his own debts.

Once my feet touch the road, and I am in the forest, I run. The temperature dips noticeably, sending a wave of chilled air over me.

It occurs to me that I don't know the exact way home, I was *asleep* for much of it. But I know the general direction, which will suffice for the time being until I hit the first town and ask someone.

After running for a solid hour, I finally allow my legs to slow to a walk. I have to make sure I save my energy for the road ahead.

Above, the birds chirp peacefully. It's hard to believe demons inhabit the forests at night. I breathe easier away from that manor and the vampire.

The day wears on, and it's a relief to just be. No need to hunt, no need to steal from the more wealthy people of town. I only need to enjoy nature and solitude.

Still, every so often—far too often for my liking—my thoughts wander back to that vampire. Surely by now, he must have returned. Undoubtedly, one of his staff will have noticed my absence and told him I've not been seen since morning.

No one has come for me. There has been nary a sound or hint of another soul on this road since I started. Mr. Devereaux must not care that I have left.

Gradually, the shadows deepen, and the once refreshing air chills further. There is still some time before the sun will set, and I must worry about demons coming out. But this damnable forest seems to be going on forever.

I might have been mistaken in slowing my pace as much as I have. I had thought for sure by now that I would have reached a town.

My stomach growls. I've been hungrier before, at least this I can ignore for the time being.

I start jogging. How long will this go on before I reach a break in the trees?

A rapid flutter of wings sounds behind me. I skid to a stop and whirl around, wondering if there's an injured bird nearby, or a small flock startled by something other than me.

Then the sound comes again, more intense, closer. I strain to listen, trying to identify it. Not a flock of birds...

I swallow.

A round of strange, yet distinct chirping, something I'd recently heard.

Shit.

That flying rodent is on my trail. No sooner do I think that then it appears through the leaves.

"Shoo, beastie! Go away!" I wave my arms at it, which doesn't do any good. It continues flying in erratic patterns, watching me with those unnerving large eyes.

It darts closer, hovering before my face. I swing at it again with my arm, but it's moving too unpredictably. It squeaks and chirps. If I didn't know better, I'd say it was trying to communicate.

"Get out of here!"

It swoops over my head and I have to duck to avoid its attack. Spinning, I ready for another attempt, but it's flying away, back toward the manor.

I watch it disappear into the distance. There is something so deliberate about that creature. Bats are not loyal things, but this one is far from ordinary.

If it came out here and returned once it found me, then Alaric must have ordered it to locate me. That means he'll soon learn I am on the road.

I turn and head off the path and into the thick of the forest, running as hard as I can to get farther away. I leap over fallen trees and swat at low hanging branches. I'm tiring quickly now,

181

but I don't dare slow down.

Fatigue grows within my muscles. I was a fool not to eat before I left, or at the very least, bring food with me.

The tip of my boot catches on the ground, and I stumble, managing to catch myself before I fall. I run and run and run until I can't catch my breath.

I have to slam into a tree to stop myself. The bark bites into the skin of my palms. Leaning against the trunk, I pant until I can breathe again.

A howl in the far distance carries to me. It's then I look around and realize how fast it's getting dark.

Seconds later, another wolf cries out, answering the call and sending a chill crawling down my spine. One more howl comes after a moment, joining them.

I stiffen. They seem to be coming from every direction. Reaching down, I grab the hilt of the stiletto dagger and pull it from my boot.

Then I'm off, running once more. I'm not sure what would be worse, fending off wolves... or higher demons. I need to get out of the forest because I do not intend to find out.

The howls chase me, growing closer the farther I run. A branch snaps close behind, and I turn to look over my shoulder.

That is my mistake.

I trip over a thick tree root protruding out of the ground and go sprawling. The impact steals my breath, and my dagger flies from my hand, landing just out of reach. At least I didn't lose it in the debris.

A twig snaps above my head, and I push myself to my knees. A man looks down at me, my dagger next to his foot. He's dressed in traditional hunting dress. Polished hunting boots, clean trousers, a fashionable jacket, and gloves. Though he seems to be missing his cap.

Light brown eyes that appear almost amber in color smile down on me. The man's auburn hair is shaggy, and the splattering of freckles across his nose and cheeks give him a youthful appearance.

He squats down, so he's eye level with me and removes his leather gloves. He holds out a hand and grins widely. "Hello, little one, what are you doing out here by yourself? Night is falling."

I don't take his hand, having seen no evidence of the horse that should be at his side. He is ridiculously handsome, but if good looks meant someone was trustworthy, I would be the best of friends with Alaric.

I lunge forward and grab my dagger at his feet and point it at his neck.

"I don't bite," he says, ignoring the sharp end and gesturing again for me to take his hand. His smile widens so much that the corners of his eyes crinkle.

We remain in a standoff, then eventually he nods and stands, taking a few steps back holding both hands up.

"I mean you no harm, little one."

"What do you want?" I ask, well aware that every second I spend dealing with him is a moment lost. The sun is setting far too quickly.

My gaze darts around for his horse. If I could take it... then I could get out of this forest before night and escape Mr. Devereaux.

"It's all right." He lists his head to the side. "I am Oliver Wolverick. You may call me Oliver, or Oli if you wish. What might yours be?"

"Clara." I narrow my eyes at him. "Clara Valmont."

"It is a pleasure to meet you, Lady Valmont."

I snort at being called a lady. One look at me is all it takes for anyone to know that.

He ignores the sound and continues, "I suppose you are looking at me because I'm dressed like a gentleman, but I'm out in the middle of the woods at sundown?"

I nod. "For all I know, you are a murderer."

"I could say the same thing about you. How do I know you won't slit my pretty throat with that dagger of yours the first chance you get?"

I ignore his question. "Where's your horse?"

"I don't need one. I live nearby—what's your excuse?"

A thought occurs to me—"You're not a vampire, are you?"

He laughs, not a quiet chuckle but a boisterous guffaw.

184

"Demons and saints, no!" he laughs. "I could not be the furthest thing from it."

I relax slightly at his seeming distaste for it.

The howling from earlier picks up once more, closer now.

"We should go," I say. "It's not safe."

Oliver steps up to me and places a hand on my shoulder. I didn't realize I lowered my dagger until just now.

"You need not fear the wolves." He leans closer and sniffs once as if he's scenting the air.

I stare dumbly at him. Of course... the howling, his sudden appearance—he's a shifter. There are none anywhere near my village, so it hadn't even occurred to me.

"I didn't realize there were any of your kind this far from the north," I say.

Oliver grins. It's a boyish smile, but it's wide enough to see his slightly elongated canines. But it fades quickly as he adopts a severe expression that doesn't quite suit him. "You smell of vampire," he says and looks around, seeming to put everything together—my being out in the forest alone, asking if he was one of them, the dagger, my obvious fear... "Are you all right?"

"I'm just trying to get home, away from one of those... monsters," I say. If he finds them as distasteful as I, then perhaps I've found an ally. "He was keeping me captive in his manor."

Oliver's eyes widen in surprise, and then he hums, saying, "I

was not aware that the vampire in these parts has become so...
primitive."

The shadows continue to lengthen, and my unease heightens.

"I need to keep going," I say.

"It's getting late. I can take you to my pack. We could always use more members."

I shake my head and move around him. I'm not interested in trading one beast for another, even if he seems nice. "I'm sorry, there is somewhere else I have to go."

Slowly, I turn my back on him and walk away. Part of me expects he will try to stop me, but I keep my dagger clutched tightly in my hand.

"Clara," he calls out. I look back over my shoulder. He hasn't moved a single step toward me. "I may not be able to protect you from the monsters that linger after sunset, but you will have nothing to fear from the wolves." He raises his arm and points in the opposite direction than I'm moving in. "You will want to head that way to the nearest town."

"Thank you," I say.

He nods, and the smile that spreads across his lips looks pitying, as though he doubts that I will make it that far.

I push my shoulders back and run in the direction he told me to go in. If I don't make it, then it won't be for the lack of trying.

CHAPTER
TWENTY-THREE
CLARA

Leaves kick up in my wake, hissing like a dozen snakes are on my heel. My imagination grows wilder and wilder by the second, spurring on my fears. The night is upon me. That thought repeats over and over through my mind with every step I take. I was hasty to leave without trying to find a map. I don't even know what direction the nearest village is.

Then a break in the trees appears up ahead, and I could almost cry in relief. I am so close to getting out, but it's too late. The demons will emerge from wherever it is they sleep during the day.

I force my legs to move faster and faster, but the brush thickens, trying to slow me down. Branches reach out, grabbing at my hair and clothes.

A flash of red glints through the dark to my right. I stumble when I look, but there's nothing there. Then another flash of red straight ahead. Two dots.

Demons.

The harder I run, the more sets of eyes seem to awaken and appear.

The shadows thicken into shapes, and I stop short as a ghastly shape rears up before me. A thick billowing cloud of black smoke slowly takes form. Its skin is too dry and taut, cracking slightly where it moves. It shows off distorted bone and ribs that stick out too far. The limbs are too long to look right.

The demon steps closer. Its form looks painful with each quick, jerky movement. The joints bend and twist in sickening directions.

I dart to the side and run. The crunching of twigs comes from directly behind me. Something cold grips my ankle and pulls. I land hard on my belly, all the air is ripped from my lungs.

The claws around my leg dig into my boots, poking through the thick leather, and twist. I cry out as pain shoots up my leg, and I'm violently jerked toward it.

It drags me over the forest floor. I scramble to grab hold of anything to stop myself, digging my nails into the dirt.

I'm losing the battle.

More demons crawl out of the shadows, their jaws snap

and crack as they come up behind the one dragging me. I swipe with the dagger, but it does no good. It lunges and grabs my leg again, giving it a swift jerk.

Something wraps around my wrist and pulls me up to my feet. At first, I think it is yet another demon, except they all vanish. Then an arm wraps around my waist. *I thought he couldn't protect me.* I breathe out and slump against my savior. "Thank you."

"You are welcome, my dear Clara," he purrs my name against my ear.

I tense. *Not Oliver.* I twist in my savior's arms and face him, and the cruel sneer marring his handsome face.

"What are you doing all the way out here?" Alaric's casual words are betrayed by the threat in his voice.

I swallow, unable to think of so much as a single word in response.

He lifts one dark brow. "Do you not understand the creatures that lurk in the forest, or are you really that foolish?"

"Let me go," I demand, but it's nothing more than a breathy whisper.

"You are my ward." His hold tightens around me. "You are my responsibility, and you won't be getting far with that twisted ankle of yours."

I shove away. He lets go without resistance. I stumble back several steps before bumping into a tree and using it to regain my balance. Each time I put weight on my left foot, sharp pains shoot up my leg.

"I'm leaving," I say. "I won't let you stop me."

He laughs, and the sound, deep and rich, makes my stomach tighten. "You wouldn't make it halfway back to that dilapidated hovel before something, or someone killed you... or worse."

"I don't care. It's better than..." my voice cracks. "You are a vampire," I say quietly. Those few simple words are enough, but it's not everything. There is much more between us than just that. There has been more than that single fact for some time now.

His face changes into the neutral mask I have come to recognize as his armor.

"Yes, my dear Clara, I am." Though the words agree, he says them with such anger... and hurt—then it's gone, and I'm not sure if I've imagined it. "But by running away, you have broken both bargains you have made with me."

"I know," I say. My fingers dig into the trunk at my back as though my life depends on it.

"What you did that day in the forest—" He takes a step closer. "What you are trying to do—" Another step. "—it is punishable by death. You are aware of this?"

I nod.

He now stands only inches away from me.

"Do you know why we have the claiming?" he asks, changing the subject.

I'm not sure where he's going with this, so I shake my head.

"To keep the humans in line. To keep you from rebelling and starting a war that you cannot hope to win. A war that would only end with your enslavement."

A war that would start if humans fought back—if we openly killed the monsters that take us, that rip our lives to shreds as if we don't matter.

"Pretty words to hide monstrous deeds," I say. "You treat us as food, tear families apart, and prey on us until everyone fears you. We are not a resource to use and throw away—and I'm not your prisoner!"

He looks at me for a long moment, his expression even, unflinching from my outburst. "I never said you were, but you killed a vampire, my dear Clara, and now we both must suffer the consequences of your actions."

I want to disagree with him, to point out every time he has made that claim... but has he?

Alaric reaches out, his fingers brushing against the base of my neck as he glides a lock of hair off my shoulder.

"I did not force this fate upon you," he says softly, his eyes staying locked on the pulse in my neck, mesmerized as he speaks. "Your father was the one who offered your sister up like chattel and you who offered yourself in her place. When I came to your home, I had no such designs to curate such a situation. I merely accepted your offer."

"I didn't have a choice," I say.

"There is always a choice." He gives me a sad look filled with pity, but there's a coldness in it. "It is lucky I found you before anyone else did."

I scoff. "You and I have very different ideas on what constitutes as luck."

"Believe me when I tell you this," he says, leaning closer still. "Your fate at the hands of another vampire would have been a long, painful, and drawn out death."

I swallow hard as he pulls back to look me in the eye.

"Alaric, please," I say, but I'm not sure exactly what I'm begging for—a quick death, or mercy, or something else entirely. "If I owe a life debt, then take it."

Alaric looks at me, and I can't for the life of me begin to imagine what is going through his mind.

He closes the small distance between us, pressing his body against mine, one hand resting on my hip, his other by the side of my head, caging me in. Even now, with these slight touches, my heart pounds, not entirely out of fear.

He lowers his head so I can feel his warm breath on my ear. "Why are you so eager to die? Do you think so little of me because of what I am?"

I think of Mother, of her face, her features that are slowly fading from memory as time passes. I can hardly remember the sound of her voice anymore. "Vampires only know how to destroy. You are all dangerous."

"So are humans, my dear Clara. Surely there is more to it than that." He moves his hand from the tree to cup my face.

"A vampire killed my mother..." *Shit...* I don't know why I admitted that out loud to him. "Kitty and I were left with only Father to take care of us." I pull in a shaky breath, forcing myself to be brave and look him in the eye.

His arm around me is strong and unmovable like a solid steel beam. The way Alaric holds me feels like a lover's embrace.

"It's okay," I say.

A thin red line encircles his irises as his fangs descend. Even now, he hesitates.

I turn my head to the side, close my eyes, and wait for the pinch of his bite as he pierces my skin, and kills me.

CHAPTER
TWENTY-FOUR
ALARIC

Instinct wins over, standing this close to her. Our chests are flush together. I can feel every breath she takes with painful precision. The pulse in her bared neck beats wildly, calling my inner demon out, taunting and luring and daring me to kill her.

I lean forward, mesmerized by her heartbeat until my lips brush her skin. My fangs scrape that same spot. That thin layer of flesh is the only thing that separates me from the thing I crave the most.

Clara tilts her head further to the side, offering no resistance. I stay like that for a moment, feeling the beat of her heart beneath my lips.

"I don't regret what I did," she says quietly. "We all do what we must for the people we love."

Following the words that nearly set my bloodlust free, is the faint scent of salt and water.

I inhale sharply and pull my head back, blinking and feeling like I am coming out of a trance.

A single tear glides down the side of her face. *She's crying.*

"Do it already, you heartless bastard."

I blink away the bloodlust as I regain my control. What a vexing creature she is turning out to be. I lift my hand and brush the strand of hair that had fallen over her face.

I can't remember the last time I saw someone cry. Brushing my thumb over her cheekbone, I wipe away the tear. Clara shudders, her chest rising and falling as she prepares herself for a death I have had every intention on drawing out as painfully as I could a moment ago, a death I no longer think I can deliver. A death I do not want to deliver.

For the first time since meeting her, I look at her—really look. The pain of having her life ripped apart is evident. My goal has been to make her suffer for her crimes, but at every attempt, all I can hear is Rosalie's voice admonishing me for my actions.

She murdered Rosalie—she doesn't deserve my pity.

Clara's pain shines through her bravado, even when she is willing to die. It tugs on me and, though I am loathed to admit it, we have something in common.

I thought I would have to spend my days and nights torturing her. But somehow in an attempt to use her repulsion of what I am against her, it became an entirely new game between us.

And what should have kept us from interacting, has become my addiction.

I curse my soft mind and heart. Rosalie's kindness that I've held dear for so long... the kindness that has kept me close to the humanity I've been clinging to since the day I was turned, has made me soft... weak.

Slowly, I release her and step back. It's several seconds before she moves.

Clara peels open her eyes and stares bewildered. Her wild, long, dark hair frames her face.

"No."

"No?" she asks, echoing me.

"I have taken nothing from you, and I do not plan on taking anything now."

She wrinkles her forehead. "I don't understand... then how am I to pay my debt?"

"Do you wish for death so desperately?" I ask. Was I wrong to think she didn't want to die? As willing, as she seemed, her tears said otherwise.

Clara drops her gaze, her features hardening. "If it is a debt I owe you, let me pay it or let me go."

"Do not tempt me, Clara." I take one more step back and lift my chin, looking down at her as though her very presence offends me... "I will take nothing from you, but that doesn't mean there's nothing I want."

There is something about her I want... her humanity.

It has been so long since I have been around mortals who were anything more than shallow worshippers that offered up their blood to have the mark of a vampire.

She shudders, her eyes sliding closed for the briefest moment. I'm not entirely sure it's from revulsion either.

She takes a few steps away from the tree, favoring her left leg. This will make the trip back long and arduous.

"I won't go back with you," she says.

"I could always return you to your home and claim your sister. Would you prefer that?"

"No, Kitty is innocent. Leave her out of this."

"The innocence of others hardly matters." I don't know if I am growing fond of her defiance or find it tiring. "You have no choice. A debt is a debt. Now come, we must leave."

I walk away from her in the direction of the manor. She doesn't follow at first, then after a moment, she does. The howling of demons growing bolder without my presence no doubt spurred her on.

"My ankle," she says. "I can do little more than hobble."

I pause to look at her. "Then, you better learn to hobble faster."

I keep up my pace, stopping every several minutes, allowing her time to catch up when she lags too far behind, and my reach to keep the demons can extend no further.

Demons and saints... The average human pace is slow enough to drive me mad, but this... this is a new agony. To her credit, she doesn't complain once.

I stop and finally look back at her upon her footsteps silencing. She stands, leaning on a tree with her weight off her left foot. Sweat glistens across her brow, and the grimace of pain tightens her features.

This woman has no sense of self-preservation whatsoever. She is behaving as though it were the middle of a bright day and not late into the night—as if we weren't surrounded by higher demons that would rip her to shreds after possessing her body and breaking her in every way imaginable.

Clara looks up and begins walking once more. Her limp is more pronounced now, and her breathing labored even as she fights to keep it slow and even.

She stumbles and falls to the ground. She presses her hands into the dirt, her fingers digging in with the strain as she tries to push herself up.

I shouldn't help her. She deserves to walk all the way back after the trouble she's caused. Nevertheless, I stride over to her and lift her up, positioning her in my arms to carry her.

"What do you think you are doing?" she asks, every muscle in her body tensing.

"It will take us all week if I let you continue on at your pace," I say, starting to walk. It's a relief to finally make some headway. What would have taken hours at Clara's pace takes me minutes.

After she adjusts to the much faster speed, she relaxes into me. Then after another moment or two, she rests her head on my shoulder.

The little fool has allowed herself to grow comfortable when I am barely able to keep myself from destroying her—it is only her humanity that keeps that dark part of me at bay.

Sharp, searing pain shreds down my back. I stumble and we fall. We collide with the ground, a tangle of limbs as the growl of a demon snarls from behind.

"Stay down," I order as I get to my feet and face the higher demon invading my territory.

It is one thing for lesser and higher demons to roam as they please, having no master. But all higher demons were once considered the most powerful of greater demons that bonded to an individual vampire. It is what grants both the demon and vampire their powers.

This was not a random attack—this nightmare was sent.

The demon morphs and changes shapes, avoiding the form it has adopted so I can't identify its master.

"Who sent you?"

I pull in a deep breath and call to my power. It curls like a viper in the pit of my stomach, ready to strike.

"Youuu arrre weeeak," it hisses. "Thissss isss gooood forrr usssss."

The abomination's red eyes lock onto Clara as it licks its nonexistent lips. It lunges. I lift my arms and send all the power I can summon to banish it. The movement does nothing, but it helps me focus the command.

Red, demonic power veins over my hands and up my arms. It rolls over my skin, snapping and cracking as it shoots out.

The demon fights against my hold, inching closer to Clara. Its large, gaping maw opens in an attack, waiting for its chance to strike.

I step to the side, placing my hands on the craggy skin, and push my powers into it.

The hardened rock-like flesh is so cold, it burns. I suck in a sharp intake of air between my teeth.

Long skeletal arms swat at me, talons digging into my back and slicing down.

I will not allow this trespass to go unpunished. I use every bit of power I possess, more than is wise, to send it away.

The demon rears up, eyes growing wide. It sways back and forth in the air. "Weee arrre nooot finisssshed," it hisses the warning.

In the sigh of a breath, its corporeal form turns into black mist, vanishing into the night to return to their master.

I have several ideas who might be responsible, but... there is no time to dwell on that now. We must get back to the manor.

I feel my strength draining as the poison of its cutting claws seeps into me.

I turn to Clara and find her cowering against a tree. Her wide eyes still staring at the spot the demon had been seconds before.

"Are you all right?" I ask, reaching a hand out to her. Her sharp eyes finally look to me. Her throat bobs, but otherwise, she doesn't speak or move. "Clara, we must go now."

She slips her icy hand into mine and allows me to help her stand. If I fall outside the manor grounds, she will be taken by any demon that is in the vicinity. We must return to the manor before that happens.

I scoop her up once more and run.

CHAPTER
TWENTY-FIVE
CLARA

He runs with me in his arms at an incredible speed. I tighten my arms around his neck and close my eyes against the dizzying blur of everything passes us by.

I find myself being lulled into relaxing against him. We make it to the manor in what could only be minutes. I expect him to set me down and leave me to find my way to my room, or yell at me for attempting to break our bargain.

But he doesn't. Alaric slows to a walk. I try to wriggle out of his arms, and he holds me tighter, carrying me until we are safely inside. He kicks the door closed with his foot and storms into the drawing room where a blazing fire awaits.

I want to tell him to let me go, but judging from the glower on his face, he is beyond furious, and I don't dare speak.

He stops next to the fireplace and releases my legs, lowering me gradually to the floor. With my hands braced on his shoulders, my body slides down his, caressing every line and muscle. My face warms.

Alaric's chest heaves as his dark eyes narrow. I can't fight the instinct that makes me back up. He advances with every step, closing the distance I create until my back presses against the wall.

"I told you," he says low and dark. "Not to wander outside at night. What part of that did you not understand?" He grabs my face with both hands and moves my head around, then takes a half a step back and looks at the rest of me. "Are you hurt?"

"No," I say, and I'm not thrilled that it comes out as little more than a breathy whisper.

He leans forward, resting his forearm against the wall next to my head. It's so similar to when he found me in the forest and yet so different. His hands gently move over me, and this time there's no anger in his posture.

My eyes flick to his mouth and linger on those full lips as he leans closer and closer. Heat washes over my body.

What is he doing?

Alaric's eyes slide closed, and I don't know if my heart thunders in my chest from anticipation or fear.

I open my mouth to protest as he leans against me. He's heavy. The warmth spreading through me seconds ago, dissipates.

"Alaric?"

When he doesn't respond, I know something is wrong.

He slumps. I manage to wrap my arms around him before he falls. There is a wet, sticky warmth where my hands touch his back.

He's hurt.

Struggling to keep him from dropping, I lower him to the ground, positioning him on his side. I crouch and carefully examine his back, moving the scraps of material to get a better view. Several long, deep gashes cover his back.

His face is pale in the firelight, and he's unconscious. For a moment, I don't know what to do. There is no way I can drag him up to the third floor to his room. I should pull the dagger from my boot and end him now.

It's the perfect chance to free myself from our bargain.

I reach my shaking hand toward the hilt and slowly withdraw it. One swift movement and this world will be rid of another vampire.

I stare at him, holding the dagger above his chest for a long moment, willing my arm to obey... but I can't bring myself to do it.

He saved me...

He had saved me from the higher demon in the forest, and he was hurt for it. The mournful cries of lesser demons grow louder from outside, sending shivers over me, and driving the point home.

I owe it to Alaric to keep him safe now.

I stand and look down at him, curled up on his side, features contorted in pain, and I feel the need to do *something*.

The demons won't come inside... they can't unless given permission. Still, their sounds fill me with a fear of them I have never known before.

I bite down on my bottom lip, not wanting to leave his side. Even with him unconscious, I feel safe in his abilities to keep them at bay.

I waver. What I need to help him is down the hall.

The demons can't enter here. The demons can't get me.

Pulling in a deep breath, I bolt out of the room, running to the kitchen. It's completely empty. Alaric said the servants were not available at night, but I had assumed that was a rule meant to punish me. I quickly grab a kettle of water, a towel, and a small bowl.

When I return, Alaric hasn't moved. I set the kettle in the fireplace kettle holder then kneel at his side. I didn't even know he'd been hurt at first. I reach out and brush his hair back off his forehead.

Plucking up the towel, I tear it into strips as the water heats. I dip one rag in, ringing out the excess water once soaked.

His shirt clings to his back, sticky and wet with blood.

I'll have to tear it open to clean his wounds. Once more, I pick up the blade, the polished metal gleams in the light cast by the fire.

With my other hand, I reach forward. Alaric's hand shoots out and grabs my wrist.

"No," he growls. There is confusion, hurt, and perhaps a little fear in his eyes. "You would cut me down... *now?*"

I pull my wrist from his grasp. He's still so strong, even as hurt as he is. I could kill him in his weakened state, I'd already thought about it. But hearing him say that makes my stomach churn.

"I will not hurt you," I say with as much calm and confidence as I can muster, grateful my voice doesn't waver.

Alaric narrows his dark blue eyes that almost look completely black now. He doesn't trust me, and why should he?

"Leave me, I will be fine," he says, his voice guttural.

He looks as if he will try to push himself up off the floor to protect himself from me. Alaric doesn't trust me, but I don't blame him, I wouldn't either.

We hold each other's gaze for several seconds before his energy fades. His eyes close again—either in defeat or exhaustion—and his head lowers back to the floor.

I brush his hair from his forehead and smooth my fingers over his pinched brow. I wait another moment to make sure he is unconscious this time, then reach over him and grip the edge of his shirt, dragging the side of the dagger across it. The cloth falls away with ease.

Setting the dagger on the floor, I fold the ripped edges of his shirt out of my way.

I dip the ripped rag back into the heated bowl of water, then look at the horrible wounds on his back and let out a hiss. I focus on the task and try not to think about the fact that it doesn't look like he's even begun to heal yet, and what that could possibly mean.

With one hand on his shoulder, I pull him closer so that his chest rests against my thighs. I press the wet cloth to his back, and his whole body goes rigid, but he doesn't wake again. I do my best to clean the area around the wounds first, moving carefully, then covering a small patch of skin at a time.

Slowly, he begins to relax against me as he grows used to my touch.

Once the area has been cleaned, I rinse out the rags and soak them again, laying them over the deep slices in his back.

I sit back on my heels and wipe my brow.

It's not the best, but it's the best I can do for now. Shifting, I straighten out my legs and rest Alaric's head in my lap. And then, I wait. For what, I'm not sure. I suppose I am waiting for him to wake or for one of the housekeepers to arrive in the morning to take care of him.

A fluttering sound from within the manor startles me, and I reach for the dagger and grip it tightly, holding it out.

The sound moves closer as my mind goes back to all the demons from the forest.

Seconds tick by, punctuated by the ticking clock on the mantle. Then to my relief, Cherno flaps into the room. The animal's movements grow more erratic than usual at seeing us on the floor, its master injured.

I drop my arm and watch the creature. It swoops down and lands a foot away then crawls over to him. It climbs up his leg and his arm, eventually settling against Alaric's chest.

Something about that touches me. This creature loves him.

Alaric's breathing seems to deepen, evening out some. The grimace of pain on his sculpted face has faded.

I watch him for a long time. My fingers find their way to his thick, silken hair, running through it in slow, soothing strokes before I realize what I'm doing. I pause briefly, but don't stop.

Asleep, he looks youthful and sweet, with no trace of the monster in sight. His skin is warm, and he's very much alive, down to the beating of his heart. The tales I have heard all my life claim vampires are like the dead. Cold, with no pulse.

He seems to lean into me as I stroke his hair, though that's most likely just my imagination. The movement seems to comfort him, so I continue.

I stay like that even when the demons grow louder then quieter as the night wears on, and even when the heavy tug of sleep pulls me down.

The next thing I know, something smooth and warm caresses my cheek. I try to open my eyes, but I can't manage more than the smallest opening. My vision is blurred by exhaustion, and my lashes weigh my eyelids down. Try as I might to fight it, sleep has wrapped me in its embrace.

The warmth that surrounded me vanishes before returning. My world shifts. I want to fight, but for some reason, I don't because I feel safe. Or perhaps I'm too tired to know to feel fear.

My body feels as though it's floating, the gentle sway lulls me deeper into my slumber until I'm placed on something cool yet incredibly soft.

As the warmth leaves me once more, I try to protest. *Don't go,* but I can't summon the energy to speak.

There's another shift, and the warmth returns, this time it's at my back as a comforting weight settles over my waist. I roll over and curl into the source.

Once more, I attempt to open my eyes and speak, but the comfort does me in, and sleep takes me.

By the time I manage to force my eyes open, the evening sun is setting through the window, and the warmth that had earlier surrounded me is gone.

I roll to my back and blink up at the ceiling.

My hand skims over the cool blankets behind me. Had I imagined Alaric here with me as I slept?

CHAPTER
TWENTY-SIX
ALARIC

A dull ache tugs on my back. I shift. The skin there is tight as it continues to heal, though the worst has passed.

I blink my eyes open. My head rests on something soft—a leg. My gaze travels along the leg, and up the feminine torso, to Clara's face. One hand is tangled in my hair, bringing vague memories of her running her fingers through it. Her other hand rests on my chest, clutching Rosalie's stolen dagger.

I am a little shocked to discover it's not pointed at me, but rather toward the door.

She had run to get away, but when she had the chance to draw blood and earn her freedom—she didn't take it.

She was protecting me. There was nothing in this house that could have harmed me, and I would have healed on my own, a fact she must have been aware of, yet still, she tended to me and stayed by my side.

She is fast asleep. I lift a hand and cup her face. The high demon of the Otherworld must have sent this woman to torture and confound me. As hard as I fight it, there is something about her that softens my heart.

Cherno's had pops up under my arm. "I thought you would never heal."

"Thank you, my friend, you have helped a great deal by lending me your power."

"What happened?" Cherno crawls up onto Clara's lap as I sit up. My powers will need several more hours to heal properly, and I will need blood.

"We shall speak of this shortly," I say quietly. "Wait for me in the study."

Cherno flits off without another word. I must have been in poor condition for them to obey without discord.

Clara's breath comes in soft sighs, though her expression is tight with worry.

I kneel and scoop her up into my arms, then pick up the dagger. She shifts and buries her face in my chest, one hand clinging to the front of my ruined shirt.

Otherworld take me. I should leave her on the floor, but I don't. I can't after she stayed with me.

I carry her to her room as she holds tight to me.

Setting the dagger on the night table, I lay her down on the bed. As I withdraw, she makes a pitiful whimpering sound and murmurs something that sounds like, "Don't go."

Leave, I tell myself. *Leave now.* But her frown deepens as she reaches out. I run a hand down my face, unable to believe I am about to do this.

I sit on the edge of the bed and stretch out against her back. The moment I am settled, she shifts to face me. I will give her this, only for a while. I lay my arm across her while attempting to keep some distance between us, but—*demons and saints*—the woman curls into me.

Yes, she was definitely sent from the Otherworld to torture me.

Time passes slowly, and I am acutely aware of every inch of her pressed against me.

What in the Otherworld am I doing holding this woman? I should want to kill her, not touch her.

Too long have I lived striving to hold on to my humanity, to be the person Rosalie believed I was.

Now hate is too foreign an emotion to hold on to. Boredom, disdain, neutrality—yes, but Clara has made it impossible to feel such paltry emotions toward her.

I understand now why she killed the first vampire she came across. It is the same reason I lived by Rosalie's rules.

"You are not at all what I thought you were, my dear Clara," I whisper.

Eventually, dawn breaks, lighting the room with a soft glow. I inch away as gently as I can and place a blanket over her.

In the study, I find Cherno hanging before the fireplace. Their large shadow is thrown across the room.

I pour a glass of blood from the carafe set out on the desk as I sit. Cherno drops, swooping up just before hitting the floor and lands on the desk before me.

"I believe I have found the cause of the increase in lesser demon activity," I say. "There was a higher demon in the forest—"

"That is impossible," they say.

"I was able to fight it off and get Clara and myself away before it did much damage."

Cherno flaps their wings, sending papers everywhere. I make an attempt to catch a few but give up quickly. "You would have died without my help, you fool."

I glare at the insult, but instead of responding, I take a sip of my drink.

"Who was it?" they demand.

I set my glass down and run a finger along the rim. "I don't know. They shifted constantly, refusing to take their true shape." Standing, I pick up the scattered papers Cherno had made a mess of and pause when I get to Elizabeth's letter. "You don't think the Queen Bitch sent it, do you?"

Cherno hisses. A strange sound coming from something that looks like a bat. "No, but she will want to see the first human you have decided to claim. Though if you leave the girl as she is, Elizabeth will kill her."

My hand tightens around the letter, crumpling it. "I will not force that on Clara. She will make the choice herself."

If it were anyone else, Elizabeth wouldn't give two shits about the human claimed. But since the day I was turned, she has attempted to dig her claws into me, and now Clara will pay with her life because I had thought I wanted revenge.

"They still don't know about Rosalie... no one does," I admit after a long silence.

"Then it is even more imperative that you mark Clara. Unless you wish to see her dead."

I pace the room. After several strides, my muscles feel weak, threatening to give out on me. I almost say I wouldn't mind seeing her dead—but that is no longer true.

Stumbling, I manage to catch myself against the wall. My breathing grows ragged and labored.

Even with Cherno's added power, healing has drained me to levels I have never felt before.

Cherno flies over and lands on my shoulder. "I am sorry, Master. I gave you what I could, now you must feed and rest."

I nod. "Find one for tonight, bring her to the atrium, and make sure she is willing. And," I add as an afterthought. "Clara's ankle is twisted—if you could take care of that. It shouldn't require much power."

With that, I straighten and head out of the office to my room down the hall.

The matter of Clara has grown complicated. I feel as though I am losing my mind when I am near her. Even after knowing what she did, I still can't seem to keep my distance. Touching her is like a drug. Though my heart and body are at war.

When I first traced Rosalie's blood to her, I thought she was nothing more than another cold-blooded killer, trying to justify her crimes so she could feel vindicated. But then she had saved that human girl, a child she didn't even know... and last night.

There were a thousand chances for her to cut me with that dagger, win her freedom, or outright kill me as she claimed she wanted to do so many times. And yet she had my unconscious form and used that very blade to protect me.

Clara must be marked... I've thought to let her draw blood so she can leave or just breaking our bargain and sending her away, but even the thought of doing so is impossible. I am too selfish, too weak.

I don't want to let her go.

Despite the roaring fire along the far wall of my room, making shadows dance as it warms the air, it feels cold and empty.

CHAPTER
TWENTY-SEVEN
CLARA

I pull in a deep breath and let it out, stretching my entire body. My legs are tired and a little sore. I sit up and look around, unsure how I got to my room...

A dull ache thrums behind my eyes, and I press the heel of my palm to my head. I need water. The last thing I remember was being in the drawing room with Alaric...

My hand flies to my mouth. *He's hurt.*

I slide off the bed, my pulse pounding in my veins. I have to find him.

Still dressed in the clothes I wore yesterday, I race through the hall and down the stairs, nearly running into the drawing room's doorframe.

The fire burns. But the bowl of water and bloodied rags are

gone. There is no evidence that Alaric and I were ever there.

I walk in and look at the wall next to the hearth where he had slumped against me, the spot where I had held him until I lost the battle to my own exhaustion.

I know I didn't imagine it. I had run and been attacked by a lesser demon. Alaric had come and somehow chased them off. I know he fought a demon and was injured. Though they both moved impossibly fast, I had watched them fight. I know I had.

My leg... I was hurt. But since I woke up, I've been walking on it. It's not even sore. I reach down and pull up the last of my trousers and look at my leg. There's no sign of bruising or swelling.

But that isn't right—I had felt the pain as that demon grabbed me and dragged me across the forest.

I make my way to the dining area to find it empty, not so much as a single cup set out. Then I make my way back upstairs to check the library, only to discover that it, too, is empty and cold for the lack of a fire. I don't even hesitate, going to the third floor. Two rooms are locked, the first I assume to be his bedroom and the mysterious room from before. I knock on each and wait, only for no reply to come.

Only his study is all that is left. The door is ajar, and there is a fire crackling in the hearth, but Alaric is not there.

He couldn't have died—but I would know... wouldn't I?

I feel as if I am the only one in this large manor. Not even the servants are around... they have probably already left for the

217

evening as the sun will set soon.

Returning to the bottom floor, I venture to the back, only to discover what I thought was a servant's area is really another hall leading to a massive music room, fit for entertaining as many people as one could want.

Much like the rest of the manor, the floors and walls are dark mahogany wood. Windows cover the two outer walls. They are grouped into sets of three with pointed arches at the top and the center window being the largest.

The vaulted ceiling is broken up into four parts, giving the feeling of separating the room into several sections, each punctuated with a chandelier made of black metal and crystals.

Large decorative rugs are set around the room. In one section, along the south side of the room, is a black grand piano, and light from the candelabra atop it glitters like gold off the polished surface. Plush couches and chairs are situated within the sections.

In each corner of the room are built-in shelves housing several books.

I wander farther into the room, and there is another hall, half-hidden behind an illusion caused by shadows and heavy drapes leading toward what I believe is the atrium.

The rich scent of roses and other flowers perfume the air. I inhale deeply and follow it, content to be momentarily distracted in my search.

As I near the glass doors, tall, lush plants block the view inside. A woman's voice drifts into the hall. I pause before the opening. Dim candlelight emanates from inside.

Near the center of the room, a large pool of water with a small fountain pours a thin stream of water from a winding sculpture of flowers and thorny vines.

The blood in my veins turns to ice. Alaric stands before it. He holds a woman tightly to him. One hand tilting her head to the side... and his mouth is pressed to her neck.

The rest of the world falls away and spots dance before my eyes, I inhale a sharp breath and blink, trying to get rid of them.

His gaze shoots up and locks on me. The slightest line of dark liquid drips down the corner of his mouth. I back up into the shadows.

"Leave," he orders her, not breaking eye contact with me, and releases her from his arms as if she were nothing.

The woman giggles drunkenly then pouts when she sees that he's done with her. Sullenly she walks away and out the glass doors into the night.

I continue to back up until I hit the wall, and even then, I press myself into it, trying to become invisible.

As soon as the doors close behind the woman, he prowls toward me. I turn and run.

I make it as far as down the hall to the music room when he catches up to me, blocking my path.

I back up, but with each step I take, he matches it with one of his own. I stop when the backs of my legs bump into one of the furniture pieces.

"What are you doing?" he snaps.

"I-I was looking for you... I was worried," I stammer.

Alaric raises his brows in surprise. "Why in the Otherworld would you be worried?"

I lift my chin and ask, "What were you doing to her?"

The thin line of blood in the corner of his mouth is still there. He takes a step closer, and I ball my hands into fists at my side, determined not to move or flinch.

Until now, he had never shown this side of himself to me. He had consumed blood before, I know he had, but it was always in a glass, where my mind could come to terms with it. Seeing him drink from that woman, her intoxicated smile as he drained her life away, makes my stomach clench.

"Why does it surprise you that a vampire would need blood to survive?" he asks mockingly, his tongue darting out to lick at the blood. His fangs show themselves in a humorless smirk. "Did you expect I would live off air and moonlight?"

"You would have killed her," I accuse him. Shock crosses his features before his eyes narrow.

I glare up into his face, meeting his gaze with unwavering steel in my own eyes. He takes one more step closer, closing what little space between us that remains, but he doesn't move to touch me.

"Make no mistake, Clara, I am every inch the monster you have known us all to be," Alaric practically purrs out, his voice sending shivers down my spine.

The way he speaks is both a threat and something deeply sensual all at once. The words caress my skin like the lightest touch of his fingers. I start to waver, shuddering at the realization that I want him to touch me.

"I'm not afraid of you," I say, meaning it. He's trying to scare me, but even now, if he wanted, he could have killed me before I could think to stop him. But he hasn't, his posture isn't even threatening, instead, Alaric looks as though he's holding himself back from something far more dangerous to us both.

And part of me responds to that part of him.

I don't think about what my life used to be, what it is now, the events that led me to this exact moment, the reasons why I should hate him, or anyone other than the man standing before me, and the way he makes heat curl in my veins.

His deep sapphire eyes darken until they are almost entirely swallowed by his pupils.

Without thinking, I lean forward and make contact with him. That slight touch is all he needs.

In a move too fast for me to see, one of his hands tangles in my hair, the other curves around my waist, and draws me into him. I can't get away, even if I wanted to.

My breath picks up at the contact. Alaric's warm breath brushes against my cheek. He tilts my head to the side, lowering his face to the crook of my neck, then places his mouth against my skin. I wait for him to bite down, but he doesn't.

"You're playing a dangerous game, Clara," he says against

me. His lips caress the sensitive spot of skin as he leaves a trail of kisses, moving up my neck to my jaw.

"I want you," I say breathlessly. I don't mean to speak out loud, but the words slip out on their own.

He lets out a low groan deep in his chest and pulls back slightly, his eyes fluttering open to meet my gaze for just a second. The heat there startles me, and I feel my own desire grow. "Your words are a sweet poison, and I can't help but drink them from your lips."

I don't know if it's him that moves or if I do, but his mouth is on mine, hungry and devouring. I melt into him. I know I shouldn't want him—he is everything I despise, and I am everything he loathes.

But I do want him. I want to lose myself in this moment, to drown in how he makes me feel, and it leaves an ache in my core.

I run my hands up his arms and lock them behind his neck. There's something about that movement that makes him pull away.

He lets go of me and backs away. We look at each other as if we are both waking from a dream.

My skin still burns with his touch and his kiss, taunting me.

"I hate you," I say, but my words lack venom.

He raises a single dark brow. "Because I am a vampire?"

I nod. "Yes."

"Yet, you stayed by my side all night, guarding me." Alaric takes me in, suspicion darkening his expression.

"And you saved me from demons," I say.

I'm unsure what this thing is between us or how I can want a vampire. I take a hesitant step forward. When he doesn't retreat, I take another step, then another. I place my hands on his chest and wait for him to turn around and leave.

He stays. His hands find my waist and pull me to him. I drag my gaze up to meet his. Neither of us attempts to move for what could be seconds or hours. He leans forward and kisses me again.

The kiss is different this time, it is different than the ones I owed to him through our bargain. This one is soft and almost uncertain. After several moments, when neither of us pulls away, he deepens it. His mouth sweeps over mine. I make a breathy sound as he coaxes my lips open, and his tongue enters.

The very taste of him is intoxicating. I press myself against him, needing to be closer. My fingers fumble with his cravat until it's undone, then I move to his vest. He responds in kind, undoing the buttons of my blouse.

The second his hands touch the bare skin of my ribs, he breaks our kiss. The hard length of him presses against my lower abdomen. Alaric's thumbs brush the undersides of my breasts, while his mouth continues trailing along my jaw and down my neck, pausing when he gets to the spot where my pulse pounds beneath my skin.

He lifts me up, and I wrap my legs around him while he continues to kiss every patch of skin he can reach, going lower and lower. I gasp as he takes the peak of one breast into his mouth.

His fangs graze my skin without piercing, sending delicious shivers all over, and all I can think about is what it would be like to have all of him pressed down on top of me.

Slowly, he lifts his head, his gaze smolders, and I almost have to look away from the sheer intensity. A million thoughts are swirling behind his eyes as he remembers himself, and as I remember everything I wanted to forget.

His hold on me loosens, and I slide down the front of his body. I don't want to stop, and I can feel he doesn't either.

"Clara," he says my name then falls silent as if he's lost for words.

I can't blame him... I am too.

Neither of us wants to say what needs to be said, though we are both thinking it. We don't break eye contact, but I release my hands from my efforts at removing his shirt as he redoes the buttons of mine.

There is far too much between us that we have not yet dealt with.

As my passion dissipates, I realize all it would take from him is a single gesture or word or look, and I would gladly give myself over to him.

And as messed up as it is to crave him as I do, I know this isn't his doing. He's not using any power on me like I wanted to think.

Whatever we have between us is fucked up. There should be nothing but animosity, but there is so, so much more.

After we have straightened ourselves, he wordlessly offers me his arm. I take it and let Alaric guide me down the hall toward the stairs.

Neither of us speaks as we walk. When we reach the door to my room, I enter and turn to face him. He remains on the other side of the threshold.

"Do you know why I gave you that particular dagger and not one incapable of harming me?" he asks, cupping my cheek with his hand.

I shake my head.

"Because I knew that you would inevitably change me before you left. And I want a reminder of it, even if it is in the shape of a scar."

There's something so dark and disturbing about that, but it's touching all the same.

CHAPTER
TWENTY-EIGHT
CLARA

The wind whips through the trees at the edge of the property as a late autumn storm rolls in from the west. Relaxing in the window seat of the library, I set the book I was reading to the side and wrap my arms around my legs, resting my cheek on my knee while I watch the tree boughs sway in the late evening light. Already the demons howling can be heard.

"Clara," Alaric says my name quietly. Turning to him, I can't help the warmth that pools in my core.

Alaric is dressed as usual, only with the addition of an overcoat in such a deep shade of red, it almost looks black. Along the ends of his sleeves and trimming the collar is an even darker material with a subtle black damask pattern.

"You're leaving," I say.

He nods. "I have business I must take care of and won't return until late."

I drop my legs off the edge of the bench, making room for him. He sits, one leg propped up so he can face me.

"Is that all?" I ask when he doesn't speak.

Even without his fangs bared or the ring of red that comes out when he wants to feed, there is something unearthly about him, something very vampire. I find that realization interesting, as the vampireness of him doesn't repulse me as it once did. In fact, it has somehow given him an endearing quality.

And while I do hate vampires because there is still one out there responsible for Mother's death... I find that I cannot hate this man as I wanted to believe I did and could.

I bite down on my lip as my breath catches. I don't know if this change is because of what happened last night in the music room or because he nearly died protecting me when I tried to run away. He was hurt because of me.

"I wanted to say goodbye before I left," he says. "And to talk to you about something else."

Alaric looks young, uncertain, and it doesn't suit him. He's avoiding saying whatever it is he has come to say, and that makes me nervous. What can he say that is so terrible that neither of us would like it?

My blood chills at what he isn't saying, and part of me dreads that he will bring up last night. Neither of us has even tried to talk about what we almost did, how far we could have gone.

"Go on." I tighten my hands into fists in my lap, my nails digging into my palms.

"Soon there will be things that happen that are outside of my control, and you will be in danger as you are unmarked..." he trails off, lifting his head. A lock of hair falls across his brow.

My heart thuds against my ribs.

"Do you wish for me to mark you? It will make it known to any others who might cross your path that they cannot lay a finger on you, and it will allow you to resist compulsion. Most importantly, it will mean that no other can punish you for killing a vampire should anyone find out."

They are all good points, I know logically that they are, especially if I want to stay alive. And there is every reason in the world to agree to such a thing.

Except one: It would mean I couldn't leave him. I could never go home to Kathrine ever again.

"No," I say quickly.

My stomach turns, watching his face fall in disappointment. "Clara, you have murdered a vampire, you know what that means. When they find out, they will punish you. Even I cannot stop them from finding out the truth. You will most likely die at their hands, and there will be nothing I can do to stop that from happening."

228

"I understand... but I can't accept a mark," I say. I twist the hem of my sleeve around my finger, over and over. Then I ask a question that has been bothering me for some time. "Why do you care so much about one vampire you didn't even know? Humans die every day at the hands of your kind."

The pain is back in his eyes in an instant—pain and anger and... heartbreak. "She wasn't just any vampire," he says after a long moment. "She loved humans, refused to even drink their blood, and it made her weak."

I finally understand his anger, his frustration. I took someone from him as a vampire had taken my mother from us.

"I didn't want to see Kitty die at the hands of a vampire like Mother did," I say. "I was only trying to protect my sister."

"So was I." His voice comes out choked and laden with emotion.

I don't know what he means at first, but then, slowly, it comes into focus. The vampire I killed had been his sister. My entire world shifts at that. I had always been so consumed by my own pain that I never stopped to think it could make me into what I hated—that there could be good and terrible vampires as there are humans.

Alaric stands abruptly. "I must go now, the hour grows late."

Then he takes his leave without another word. I want to stop him and say so many things, but saying *I'm sorry for killing your sister* seems far too inadequate a sentiment. At any rate, he's gone before I can even begin to find my voice.

I stay at the window seat for a while longer before roaming the manor, too distracted to read, and too guilty to eat.

"Miss," Elise's voice startles me.

I spin to face her.

"Will you be having dinner tonight, Miss?"

"No, thank you," I say, backing away, needing space to think more.

"The others and I will be staying late tonight, as the Master requested if you need anything."

"Thank you," I say as I begin walking again in the direction I came from.

"The gardens are lovely this time of night," she says quietly.

I smile wanly. "Thank you, but I don't think I will be leaving the manor, it is almost dark."

Again, I am stopped in my tracks as she speaks again. "The atrium is also lovely."

My patience growing thin, I give her the best smile I can—strained as it is—and nod. There are only so many times I can thank her for unnecessary suggestions that distract me from the thoughts weighing heavily on my mind.

Finally, she bows and goes on her way.

Letting my mind wander, my feet move of their own accord. It's not until I am in the expansive music room again that I come out of my thoughts and look at my surroundings.

My face warms, remembering how Alaric's hands glided over my skin, the way his mouth felt on mine...

I hurry through the room and nearly run down the hall, stopping at the glass doors. When I pull them open, warm, humid air hits my face in a soft wave.

I'm instantly surrounded by the scent of roses and many other exotic flowers I don't recognize. Botany was never a subject I excelled at, but their combined fragrances are beautiful. Oil lamps are placed sporadically throughout, making this feel like a cozy, sanctuary far removed from the world.

Plants of all kinds line the glass walls, and a cobblestone path winds its way through the space. At the center of it all is a raised pool with a floral sculpture pouring fresh water into it.

On the far end, there's a thin wrought iron, spiral staircase leading to a suspended balcony that encircles the entire room for yet another layer of plants. Thick vines climb up the stairs. About halfway up, between one floor and the next, is a clear view of the night.

I walk along the path, around the outer edges, and follow the long way to the pool in the center. I dip the tips of my fingers into the cold water as I pass, creating ripples that wake out.

I place my foot on the bottom step and grip the railing as it sways gently. It's old, and the lack of use makes me wonder who takes care of the plants above, and how. I place my foot on the next step up—this one stays firmly in place. After climbing a few more steps, it seems to only be the first that is loose.

Outside, the landscape is bathed in silver light as the full moon hangs heavy in the sky, drowning out the stars.

I stare outside, my gaze unfocused and unseeing. All I can think about is Alaric, the way he kissed me, the way he looked uncertain, how he asked to mark me, and how I had ruined his life. I had done what I was so afraid of having happen to him: the one person I have left in the world, taken from me.

But that's precisely what I did to him.

It's unforgivable.

In the end, I was the one who turned out to be the monster. I don't even know how Alaric can stand to look at me or want to touch me or be in the same space without ripping my throat out.

I lean back on the railing and take a deep breath in then let it out.

Everything shifts, and I am falling. I grab at the railing, but before I can register what's happening, the metal clink of it hitting the ground echoes loudly. The metal moans beneath me as the steps bend out and down. My equilibrium shifts. I can't tell which way is up, and all I can do is grab at anything to catch myself.

Time slows. My fingers claw at nothing until I catch a bent section of the railing. As I close my grasp, time speeds back up. The metal groans again, bending further from supporting my weight.

I look down. If I fall, it will hurt like hell, but I don't think it will kill me—at least I hope it won't. My heart is a deafening beat in my ears.

I cry out as the part I cling desperately to shifts again. Using every bit of strength I have, I reach up with my free hand and try to grab onto something more substantial.

One second, I am hanging, suspended in the air, the next, there's a loud crack, and I'm falling.

I hit the ground, but it hardly registers as my head cracks against the stone.

Stars explode across my vision as pain lances through my skull. I lay gasping for breath and wait for the agony to lessen. I roll to my side. The world moves in unsettling ways as though I'm on a small ship in the middle of a stormy sea.

I turn my head and retch. Each violent movement causes another series of stabbing pain to roll over me.

Eventually, I settle, lying on the cold stone ground.

I don't know how long I lie here, only that some time passes before I can gather myself and sit up without feeling sick from the pain.

Somehow, I manage to get to my feet, though it takes a lot of effort. My entire body feels bruised and beaten.

"Miss!" Elise's voice cries out from the entryway, and I cringe at the shrillness of it. She hurries to me and grabs my arm to help steady me. "What happened, Miss?"

"The railing broke when I was climbing up," I say.

"What were you doing up there? Those old stairs are rickety and dangerous," she says, and I manage to hold the sharp reply on the tip of my tongue. "Come, Miss, let's get you somewhere I can get a look at you."

I don't have the will to argue with her that I don't need her to check me out. I only need to lie down.

Once we make it across the manor to the stairs, I know I won't be able to climb. So instead, Elise leads me to the drawing room.

I lean back in the chaise lounge and sigh, glad to be off my feet. The fire crackles and dances in the hearth, and I let my eyes slide closed.

CHAPTER
TWENTY-NINE
CLARA

"I brought you tea, Miss. You had a close call," Elise says as she enters the drawing room.

My eyes snap open. I must have fallen asleep. With some effort, I manage to sit upright.

I watch Elise pour the tea then add a single lump of sugar and a splash of cream. My muscles ache in this position, so I stand, feeling the need to test my body to see if there are any serious injuries.

Moving around doesn't feel as bad as I feared it would.

"Drink up, Miss," she says, holding the cup out to me.

The tea's herbal scent is overpowering, and I honestly don't think I can stomach much at the moment. However, I take a sip to be polite. I know Elise went to some effort, no matter how small, making it for me. Hitting my head must have affected me more than I realized because even the tea seems off. I go to set it down, but she frowns.

"What is this?" I ask.

"Drink more, Miss. It will help you feel better, I promise. It's Mrs. Westfield's special blend," she says sweetly. She flits around the room, straightening pillows on the chaise lounge and other menial tasks.

I take a few more sips until I cannot stomach another drop.

Elise watches me curiously. It makes me wonder how awful I must look right now. "You should finish—"

"I'm sorry, I can't right now... please give me a few moments." I walk over to the large window and push aside the thick, heavy material of the curtain to rest my forehead against the cold glass panes and gaze out into the night.

A wave of unsettling vertigo washes over me. My fingers curl into the thick velvet as I wait for the feeling to pass.

Turning back to the room's interior, my vision wavers, and I press a clammy hand to my forehead. I blink several times, trying to clear the blur from my eyes. I'm feeling worse by the second, and it makes me glad I have nothing else in my stomach to purge.

When the world manages to right itself once more. Elise remains standing in the same spot as before, her arms now crossed over her chest, and she's watching with a strange intensity.

"I promise, I will be fine," I say, dismissing her, even though I don't know if that's true.

"It would have been better if you'd finished your tea," she says quietly.

My head is swimming. Her face goes in and out of focus.

"I think I need to sit down," I murmur. Making my way back across the room, using the wall to steady me. "I'm not feeling well." For the first time in so long, I feel entirely helpless. I'm desperate for some sense of safety and comfort. I wish—

The thought is cut off, and my blood turns to ice as I watch the cold smile spread across her lips.

Elise reaches toward the fireplace mantle. She grabs something and drags it along the top, making a horrible scratching sound against the wood.

Firelight gleams off the night-forged silver blade. I swallow hard as my mouth goes dry.

"What are you doing?" I rasp.

She waves the dagger back and forth in her hand, testing the weight of it. "At first I thought you might be good for the Master. He has never taken part in the claiming, but when he arrived with you, I thought that maybe it would be easier for him, to have a meal on hand rather than having to deal with those annoying girls who want him for the status a mark brings."

She presses the tip of her first finger to the point of the blade, then lets out a soft hiss and sucks on the wound.

I try to stand, but my muscles are sluggish and respond clumsily. I only make it halfway up before my legs give out on me, and I drop back down.

"This is sharp," she says almost absentmindedly before continuing. "But then," Elise says, pacing before me, entirely unconcerned with my efforts. "The Master never marked you. He gave you everything and look at how you repay him." She whirls to face me, pointing the dagger at my chest. "You try to kill him, and with Rosalie's dagger at that."

"You don't know what you're talking about," I grind out through clenched teeth.

It all rushes back to me in a tidal wave. The looks she gave me, how she defended Alaric when I first arrived, her outbursts, and countless other instances that had seemed benign at the time.

"I know he did everything for you, and you are ungrateful. Do you know how many women would die to be in your shoes? He deserves a loyal human, someone who will love him."

"It's not what you think. He is not my enemy," I say, trying to talk her from her plan to kill me. "We are friends." I'm not sure how true that is, but it's close enough.

"Shut up!" she snaps, her cool demeanor slipping. "You don't deserve to be claimed by him."

"And I suppose you do?" I say derisively. She's no better than the other girls she looks down on—the ones who see the mark of a vampire as a symbol of status.

"I have been serving him all my life. Since I was old enough to walk, my mother trained me to be his. I deserve to be claimed."

I don't know a lot about injuries, but my gut is screaming that something is wrong. I should be feeling better by now, not

238

progressively worse. My limbs tingle, becoming harder and harder to move, and my eyelids are heavy. I look from her to the half-drunk tea. Understanding dawns.

"You drugged my tea," I say. My words slur slightly.

Breathe… breathe and focus.

"Yes," she says without the slightest hint of emotion, then goes back to playing with the dagger. It's more than clear by now that she means to kill me. I have to keep her talking until whatever she gave me wears off.

I close my eyes for a moment and will my body to regain control.

"I have seen you," she says. "Practicing with this." She waves the dagger as if I wasn't aware of what she meant. "While you lack technical ability, you do have more training than I do. I needed something to slow you down, so I can finally be rid of you."

One word sticks out. "Finally?"

"Yes," she sighs dramatically and collapses in the chair across from me. "I had hoped that when you cut yourself, he would have fed on you until you were nothing but a dried-up corpse."

"And the atrium," I say. I wriggle my fingers and toes as feeling starts to return to my muscles, small movements to avoid drawing her attention.

"Yes, it was easy enough to borrow a tool from Mr. Steward. Though it was a gamble, you would even climb the stairs at all. Though I had hoped you'd climb to the top before falling." Elise stands and stretches.

"What have I done to you to make you want to kill me?" I ask, trying to sound as wounded as possible.

I can feel my anger starting to boil over, but rather than spit out the venomous words on the tip of my tongue, I use them to burn away at the poison and clear my head.

She lifts her chin and dons a haughty air. "You tried to kill the Master."

"I—"

"You tried to kill him," she says again, but this time there's something wild and unpredictable about her. "And instead of getting rid of you like the trash you are, he gives you more special treatment." Her voice cracks as her large blue eyes fill with tears. "I love him—you should have loved him, but you are ungrateful and undeserving."

In another life, another world... another situation, I could almost feel pity for her and the unrequited love she feels for Alaric. But not now, not when she is too cowardly to admit her feelings to him, to do anything she could have and instead take it out on someone who has no bearing on whom he loves.

It's the moment the first tear slides down her pale cheek that I know my time is up.

"Why won't you die already?" she practically screams the words at me.

I take a deep breath and prepare myself.

Her face adopts a wholly blank expression, and then she lunges for me.

CHAPTER
THIRTY
CLARA

Elise lunges for me, the dagger pointed out and away as her free hand aims for my neck. She would prefer to strangle me until my life leaves my body than deliver a quick death.

I throw myself to the side, falling to the floor and rolling away. When I come to a stop, Elise's face turns a bitter shade of red.

This time when she throws her body at me, the dagger is pointed at my chest. I kick out, my foot striking her in the stomach. She lets out a groan and stumbles sideways.

I scramble to my feet, my legs shaking. I have but a second to prepare myself for the next attack when she comes again. This time, I grab her wrists and pull them out to the side.

The sharp edge of the blade drags against my forearm as she screams her frustration. Blood, hot and sticky, runs down my arm. I let out a hiss of pain. Elise flicks her wrist, again and again, slicing at my arm at the odd angle.

More and more blood runs down my arm, and I feel the effect of further injury. I push her as hard as I can, stumbling back several steps to gain distance.

I don't get far before she is coming at me again, the dagger slicing the air. I retreat, holding my arms in front of me and blocking her from striking me in the face or chest. But with each swing of the weapon, a new slice forms across my skin. Again and again and again and again.

Blood soaks my arms and sleeves, and each cut solicits another cry of pain from my lips. I can't take much more.

Desperate for a reprieve, I drop to a crouch and kick out my leg, swinging it toward hers, catching her ankle and knocking her to the floor.

The dagger clatters on the hardwood floor, red staining the blade. I make to grab it, but she recovers too quickly, and the drink she gave me still lingers in my system, slowing my body but not my mind. With no hope of reaching it before her, I reach out and grab hold of her as her arms are outstretched.

I pull myself over her and press my weight down. Elise manages to roll to her back, dagger in hand before I can get her arms pinned. For several long seconds, neither of us move.

Then her eyes are wild and unseeing. She is once more

fighting against me, screaming.

"I love him, and you could not care less for him! You tried to hurt him... and still, he chose you!" She spits, and it hits the side of my face. "You deserve to die!" Her voice cracks, her pain a nearly tangible thing.

Then she begins to weep. I don't ease off, though she squirms and tries to get out from under my hold.

We struggle for several more moments until she realizes she is unable to stab me. Elise drops the dagger and jerks on her wrists, made slick by my blood.

She grabs hold of me now and digs her fingers into the wounds she has inflicted. My breath is sucked from my lungs, and I can't move as the world spins. She takes advantage and throws me to the side.

I heave, my stomach churning from the pain.

Elise recovers the dagger and straddles me as I lay on my back. The drug in my system will be my undoing.

Wrapping both hands over the hilt, she holds the dagger high in the air and thrusts downward. I reach up and wrap my hands around her wrists. The end of the blade hovers a few inches above my chest. She presses down harder, leaning her weight into it.

My arms shake with the effort.

I am losing.

The drugs, combined with the blood loss, have weakened me. Spots gradually form before my eyes, and I know the end is coming. If I stopped fighting right now, that dagger would plunge into my chest, and it would be over.

She is screaming, but the words have lost all meaning and have become guttural shrieks of pure rage.

My grip on her arms is slipping, the dagger is inching closer and closer until the point presses down on my chest. I grit my teeth as it begins to pierce my skin. Little by little, it digs further in, crimson forming around the tip.

A light brush of air swirls around the room then her weight on top of me is gone. The dagger is gone. My cry dies on my lips, and my arms fall limply to the floor. I suck in deep breaths.

Elise cries out, a sound more of surprise than pain.

My head lists to the side, my energy completely spent. Glittering pools of blood form under my arm. Lethargically, I lift my gaze to see a pair of men's legs. I look up, up, up to Alaric standing over me, holding Elise by the arm, his eyes are locked on mine, taking in my state.

The red ring that appears around his irises when he smells blood has swallowed the pools of blue entirely. His face distorts in a look of pure rage as he finally turns to her.

Alaric slams her against the wall, his hand moving to her neck. "You dare to be so bold in my house?"

She whimpers, her fingers clawing weakly at his hands.

He will kill her. I'm sure of it.

"You are only a servant, and yet you think you can take matters that affect me into your own hands," he snarls, and even from here, I can see his long fangs as he speaks.

"I did it for you..." she says, tears streaming down her face. The madwoman from only moments ago is gone and left in her place is a woman whose heart is breaking. "That bitch would have killed you."

Alaric's eyes narrow. "Do you think me so weak as to be so easily killed?"

"I-I did this for you." Her arms fall limply to her side. "I love you."

"You will die for your transgressions." He tilts her head to the side, exposing her neck. Her words go unheeded. He readies himself then sinks his fangs into her.

"No," I croak. I reach out for him, but I'm not close enough to stop him, and I'm too weak to get up. "Alaric..." He stiffens at the sound of his name. "Don't kill her."

He turns to me, bemused. Blood leaks from two puncture wounds in Elise's neck, but she doesn't move, as if she's waiting for him to continue.

"Please... don't kill her," I say. I have every reason to not plead for her life, every reason to want him to end her. But I can't lie here and watch this.

His eyes narrow as if he's questioning my sanity. Then to my surprise, he takes a step back and releases her. Elise slumps to her hands and knees.

"Go," he says, baring his teeth at her. "If you ever return, I will not be so lenient."

A pitiful sob breaks from her lips as she stands. Elise takes one step toward Alaric, but he turns his back on her. She buries her fists in the folds of her skirt then hurries out of the door.

Alaric is at my side in a blink. "Clara..." he says.

He looks as if he has a million things to say but can't put his thoughts into words. Alaric rips the sleeves of my shirt and wraps my arms to stanch the bleeding. The red that had swallowed up his irises has diminished to a thin ring.

I smile up at him, and say, "I'm all right."

He laughs derisively.

When he finishes with the makeshift bandages, he lifts me up into his arms and cradles me against his chest.

I nearly fall asleep before we reach my room.

My eyes fly open as he shifts me, my hands gripping onto his shirt. Alaric pauses his movements, giving me time to realize he's only setting me into my bed.

There's a rapid fluttering, and Cherno appears on his shoulder, looking at me as if the animal can understand and assess the situation.

Alaric sits on the edge of the mattress and takes one of my hands in both of his. I know he has questions, but I am in no state to answer, though he can piece it together well enough.

He's quiet for a long time, but I don't mind. The feel of his fingers caressing my hand is relaxing, and I feel safe.

"I'm sorry, we cannot heal this. The wounds were made with night-forged silver, which opposes our powers. It will take everything just to stop the bleeding so it can begin to heal."

I give him a weak smile. "Thank you."

"I had not meant to place you in harm's way," he says.

"This isn't your fault," I say. There's no way he could have known she would go that far or felt that way about him.

He assists me as I push myself to sit up.

"I am responsible for her actions—she was in my employ." Then he lifts his gaze to meet my own, the corner of his mouth ticking up. "I promise, my dear Clara, if you are to die, then it will be at my hand and my hand alone."

"Is that supposed to make me feel better?" I ask.

He raises his brows. "Does it?"

I think about it for a moment, studying his face, then nod once. "Yes, a little."

CHAPTER
THIRTY-ONE
CLARA

I glance up to the window on the third floor. The room is dark, but I know Alaric is there. Though I wish to be alone to sort through the events of last night, his presence gives me some measure of comfort. He is my strange and dark guardian.

Turning my arms over, I look at them as if I can see through my sleeves and the bandages under, to the thin skin barely healed over and just enough to have stopped the bleeding. It is still tender and raw, but I am still in awe of how much he was able to heal me.

The distant whinny of horses comes from down the road. My head snaps up.

Two white stallions come charging over the crest of the hill and down the drive. Their hooves thunder, and behind them trails a large black carriage with gold embellishments. The animals are wild, and it might be my imagination, but I can almost swear that their eyes glow a demonic red.

Chills run down my spine, and I stand and run a few steps toward the house, but the blood loss from last night has me weak and spots form, dancing before my eyes. I am forced to slow.

I only make it halfway up the steps to the front door before the carriage comes to a violent halt. I turn and face the visitor. Whoever it is, I know it cannot mean anything good for me.

The door swings open, and a beautiful man steps down, every movement is graceful in an unearthly manner that only a vampire is capable of.

His long blond hair is pulled back at the nape of his neck. He is dressed in clothes so fine that I believe he might outrank Alaric in the vampire hierarchy.

The second his eyes land on me, a broad, sensual smile spreads across his face, which leaves me with the image of a starving man seeing a banquet for the first time. I blink, and he stands only inches before me, hazel eyes ringed in red. He leans in close and inhales a deep breath then says in a whisper, more to himself, "My, you are a delicious snack, aren't you little human."

My heart beats fiercely against my ribcage.

"I am Mr. Harkstead, but you may call me Lawrence," he says as he lifts my hand and brushes his lips across my knuckles.

Distantly, I hear the sound of the door opening behind me, followed by soft footfalls. A firm arm wraps around my shoulders from behind and pulls me up against a solid chest.

"Hello, Lawrence. We hadn't expected you for a few days yet," Alaric's voice rumbles in his chest against my back.

Lawrence smiles, showing his white teeth and sharp canines. He lifts one shoulder and shrugs, his attention solely on Alaric now, though I find little comfort in it as Alaric pulls me tighter into his hold.

"Elizabeth was anxious to hear an update from you as you've failed to respond to any of her letters."

I feel Alaric stiffen at my back, and I wonder what it was about that statement that seems to worry him.

"Come," Lawrence says, "let us get out of this dreadful sun. It's too draining for my liking."

Finally, Alaric loosens his hold as he steps around me, simultaneously placing himself between the new vampire and me. "Of course, forgive my lack of manners. Come in, we will get you settled, then we can talk tonight in the study."

Mrs. Westfield bows to him, giving him a warm, familiar smile as she ushers him inside. Alaric takes my hand in his, and we follow after.

"I will be with you shortly, Lawrence, I must take care of some business first," he says, not bothering to look back as he leads me down the hall a little too fast.

"Certainly, and take your time," Lawrence says, meaning dripping from his tone. "I am in no hurry."

Once we round the corner, Alaric slows, but he doesn't speak or relinquish my hand. I want to ask him so many things, but I allow him to pull me through the manor wordlessly. Anything I say in the open can be overheard by Mr. Harkstead.

He marches me up to my room, and only then, when the door is closed, does he finally release me. Something dark shadows his features even as the tension melts visibly from his shoulders. His gaze drops to the floor.

"Clara," he whispers my name with such desperation that I cease breathing as I wait for the next words to fall from his lips. "You will not be safe outside this door. Without my mark, nothing is stopping another vampire from taking your blood."

"What does he want?" I ask.

"I have some idea, but there is something else to his presence besides simple orders." Alaric straightens and takes a step forward. His palms slide over my shoulders and down my arms. He grasps my hands in his, and I can only look at his thumb drawing slow circles along my wrist. "Will you do me the favor of staying in here as much as possible?"

"Am I to be held prisoner in my rooms then?" I ask. It is one thing to be here at all, away from Kitty. It is another to be locked up.

Alaric runs a hand through his thick, black hair. There's something in that simple gesture that makes him look absolutely powerless. "No, never. You are free to roam this floor and the library. I will have Mrs. Westfield bring your meals to you. But I implore you to try to remain hidden until they leave."

A shiver courses over me, sending goosebumps along my skin. "They?"

"More vampires are coming. Harkstead is only the first to arrive. Please," he says, one corner of his mouth twitching downward. "Please consider—"

My stomach turns into knots. "No. I cannot. You know I cannot."

"It would keep you safe," he offers.

I shake my head vehemently, taking a few steps back.

"At least think about it. Consider it as a possible option."

"Fine," I say. "I will *think* about it."

He has given me plenty of reasons before why I should accept the mark and while I do understand them, the thought of someday possibly returning to Kathrine has me keeping my refusal firmly on my lips. I think he understands, so he accepts my compromise, but I think he knows my mind is already made up.

I do feel safe with him, but if I let him near me, I fear I will give into his wish to mark me.

After several hours of keeping to my room and pacing, eating the meal brought to me, and even attempting to sleep early, I lay awake on my bed staring at the ceiling. I managed to sleep for a few hours in small bursts of time, broken by my rapid heartbeat thundering against my ribcage. The thought of this stranger coming into my room to kill me when Alaric can't get to me in time...

But those were only dreams—*nightmares*.

The wax candle on my bedside table flickers. I couldn't bring myself to snuff it out as if this small flame could do anything to protect me against a vampire.

I am free to wander this floor and the library. It seems like the only viable option for me. It might do me some good to read and let my mind focus on other things besides the uncertain. Most of all, I will not allow myself to become a prisoner here by my fears.

Slowly, I open the door to my room and peek out into the hallway. Tallow candles burn, casting a soft golden hue along the walls. All seems quiet, so If Alaric and Mr. Harkstead are up and about, they aren't in this wing of the manor.

I loose a sigh, and into my room, closing the door firmly behind me.

One door to the library is ajar. I squeeze myself through the opening, trying to stay as quiet as possible. A fire roars in the enormous hearth, and other than the snap and popping of the burning wood, I don't hear a sound.

Satisfied, I make my way through the shelves, stopping when I get to a title that catches my eye. I pull the book out and open it. There's a slight hint of dust from disuse, but under that is the scent of parchment and ink.

The clock above the fireplace chimes a late hour.

I read a few pages, standing where I am. My eyes ache. Too

tired to read, but too wound up by nerves to sleep. I close the book and return it to its spot.

"Ladies ought not to walk around strange houses at night," a dark voice croons from behind me.

I spin, pressing my back against the shelves. Immediately, a flush burns its way up my neck at being caught in my nightclothes, which earns a pleased smile from my late night visitor.

"Don't you know that's when the monsters come out to play?" Mr. Harkstead's smile broadens, showing off his long, pointed fangs.

"I couldn't sleep, and Alaric said I was welcome in the library." I hate the waver in my voice.

He studies me then gives a curt nod as if deciding on something.

"I suppose," he says. He steps around me and trails a finger across the book spines, pretending to browse. "Someone like you would really enjoy having access to the finer things in life for a change. Surrounded by riches, all of a sudden must make it quite difficult to sleep at night." He stops walking and turns to face me, an over-exaggerated scandalized expression on his pretty face. "Or is it *Mr. Devereaux* you are hoping to get a glimpse of? You are awfully familiar with him."

I know by his tone what he's implying. I was informal when referring to Alaric. But I choose to address the fact that he's insinuating I am here because I was tired of being poor, that I wanted this, not because of a debt but because I am desperate and greedy for a life beyond a normal human's ability to procure.

My face burns with my temper. "I couldn't care less about any of this." I spread my arms out, motioning to the library and the manor itself. "There's nothing he owns that would make me happy."

He raises a single brow and advances, stalking toward me like a predator with languid and graceful movements. "Then, tell me little human, what would make your mortal heart happy?"

Nothing. I think. There's not a single thing in this world that could bring me joy. Things matter little to me, and the people I know are horrible—except for Kitty and Xander.

I can't remember a time when I wasn't fighting just to survive, let alone a time when I felt happy. Though I must have been at some point. My gaze flicks to the shelf beside me. Except when reading, when I allow myself to get lost in a book.

This stranger, this vampire, leans forward and inhales a deep breath. I shudder to think why. He tugs the collar of my gown to the side, and his eyes widen.

"Well," he says. His eyes flash with a spark of red. The power infused in his voice makes my head pound. "This is a pleasant surprise. Perhaps you would like to play a game with me?" his voice echoes in my head, making it pound.

I lift my hand to swat him away, but the library doors are flung wide, and Alaric steps through the shadows. Anger sears across his perfect features, making him look like a stranger instead of the man I've come to know.

Mr. Harkstead moves away, but not far enough for my comfort.

Alaric strides over to us, looking down his nose at me. The disdain in his eyes takes me aback. Mere hours ago, he was worried about my safety and wanting me to accept his mark.

"It is late, Clara. You should consider retiring to your room for the night."

I don't argue but take the escape he's offering. I push past his guest, who sighs wearily.

"Run little human. Hide. The others are coming, and they are far more dangerous than even I..." Mr. Harkstead calls out.

"Stop that," Alaric bites out.

"You never let me have any fun," he pouts.

"You need to leave," Alaric's voice booms through the room.

"I will be doing no such thing any time soon."

My chest heaves. The mark could protect me. But what good would it do if I lose my chance at freedom? I would be here forever, and it would not be by my choice.

I am down the hall before I can hear any more, my feet padding softly on the carpeted floor.

CHAPTER
THIRTY-TWO
ALARIC

"I told you to stay away from her."

Lawrence Harkstead smiles like the cat that ate the canary. "Oh, but she promises to be a delicious little snack."

"Meet me in the study in five minutes. I must deal with her," I bite out, then turn on my heel, and hurry after Clara.

I reach her door just before she manages to close it and press my hand against it, not enough to force it open but enough to keep it from being closed in my face.

"Clara." As soon as I say her name, the pressure against the door ceases and two heartbeats later, opens wider. She steps to the side and allows me inside.

The urge to wrap my arms around her is immediate, but with

her pinched brows and lips pressed into a tight line, I know that isn't what she needs.

"I'm sorry," I say, but my words don't have the intended effect. After what happened with Elise, tonight with Lawrence was just one more blow to her safety. Though he hasn't caused her harm, the threat he made was enough.

She's strong and will heal, but Clara needs time. Clara retreats, angling her body away from me. I take half a step forward and halt when she visibly cringes.

"You should have been safe. I failed to keep my promise that it was a place you could go without worry."

Clara wraps her arms around herself, her shoulders hunched.

To look at her now, she has the wild eyes of an injured wolf being cornered, unpredictable, and ready to lash out.

"When I found you on the floor bleeding... that was not your doing, was it?" I ask.

She shakes her head.

"Why didn't you tell me?"

She doesn't speak for a long moment then raises one shoulder in a half shrug. I want her to answer, but I can see she is in no state to be pushed, so I let it go.

At least now I know it wasn't an attempt to get away from me. That fact eases me somehow.

I pull the dagger from my boot. I had meant to give it back to her after last night, but she hadn't asked for it, and part of me had hoped she wouldn't want it or need it. "Take this and keep it on you at all times, my dear Clara."

Her large brown eyes rise from the dagger to mine. Clara doesn't move for several heartbeats, then she reaches out with slow, careful movements, wrapping her fingers around the hilt and lifting it from my palm. I drop my hand as she clutches it to her.

"Will you be attempting to draw blood tonight?"

Clara startles, blinking at me in bewilderment. A crooked smile slowly forms across her full lips. The bargain is still in effect.

She steps up to me, closing the distance. She makes a soft humming sound as she lifts the dagger between us and slides the point across my chest.

Indecision wars in her eyes. She's debating. If she tried, she would fail, a fact we both know—unless I let her. It is a thought I don't want to contemplate, but it seems to be the only viable solution to get her somewhere safe.

"No," she says. The word is dry and forced. "Not tonight. I am exhausted."

With all her talk of leaving, she chose not to. And we both know I would not have stopped her this time.

I can't even begin to let myself contemplate what this means.

"Things will not get easier for you anytime soon," I say.

She nods. Simple and decisive.

Her ignorance at the matter sparks my irritation. So I say, "I can't be at your side all of the time to keep them from you."

"I understand," she says.

"Have you considered the mark?"

"I can't." She lifts her chin, setting her jaw in determination. "I can't take the chance I'll never see Kitty again."

She is a fool. I nearly say as much but manage to stay my tongue when I catch the hope glittering in her eyes.

Then I bow my head and turn toward the door. I must go and deal with Lawrence.

"Thank you," she says in a soft whisper.

I turn to look at her over my shoulder. She stands a little taller. What in the Otherworld am I going to do with her?

"We will speak again soon," I say, then take my leave, closing the door quietly behind me.

Then a soft whisper floats through the door, and I'm not sure if she means for me to hear it or not. "I won't accept a victory even if you try to cheat by handing it to me."

I don't understand this thing I have with her. Over the last several weeks, we have somehow formed a tenuous trust between us.

As much as I know I should hate her, that notion has long since left me. I find it impossible to hate what I desire.

If what nearly happened those few nights ago is any indication, she wants me as well.

But there are things far too important between us that have yet to be put to words.

I pour two glasses of brandy and hand one to Lawrence. He takes it and swirls the liquid around and around. The ice clinks lyrically against the glass as he lounges back on the sofa, feet propped up on the cushion near the fire.

I look out the window at the grounds below, bathed in the light of the silver moon. Scowling at the night, I place an arm against the pane, resting my forehead against it, then take a slow sip of my drink.

The weight of an arm slides onto my shoulder. I turn to glare at the man at my side, looking for all the world as though his presence here was because he wanted my company and not because he was sent by the queen bitch herself.

"What is the real reason you are here, Lawrence?" I ask.

He takes a sip of his drink. Pulling a face, he says, "This might be the finest brandy made, but it is deplorable next to fresh blood." He swirls his drink again before downing the remainder. "Your scent was on her, but not as it should be."

I throw my head back and swallow my drink in one gulp. "Leave it be, Lawrence."

Lawrence walks to the fireplace and leans on the mantle,

staring into the fire. He is restless tonight, and that is never a good sign. "You've not marked her yet. Elizabeth will not be happy."

"Just answer the damn question."

"You know why I'm here, Alaric. Don't play stupid. You've never claimed a human before. You had to know Elizabeth would be interested in who managed to catch your attention after all these years. If you had drank her blood and killed her, I could report that, and we could be done with this whole mess. But you haven't." He turns his piercing gray eyes on me, accusingly.

"It's pointless for her to make a fuss. Clara has nothing to do with her."

"She lives with you as if she were more than a claimed human. You not only haven't bothered to drink from her sweet little veins, but you've refused to mark her. That makes her fair game for any vampire that comes within five miles of her."

A low, warning growl rumbles up from my chest. I know it's a mistake the second it fills the room. I take a deep breath and try to regain my composure. "She doesn't wish to be marked, and I will not force any part of this life on her or anyone for that matter."

"You already forced this life on her the second you claimed her," he snaps back.

I want to lash out at him for saying as much, but it is the truth.

Lawrence narrows his eyes. "I don't know what is going on between you two, but your behavior toward her is strange for a vampire, even for you. She is only a human."

"There is nothing between us." I focus on keeping all trace of emotion from my face.

Lawrence throws his glass into the fire. The flames jump and brighten then return to normal.

"Demon shit." He runs a hand over his face then huffs out a deep sigh, resting his fists on his hips. "I won't say she is unmarked, but I do have to report that you have a human with you, alive. And you know that Elizabeth will expect you both to be there in two months' time with the rest of us. Your solitary bullshit won't work as an excuse any longer."

"I see no reason to go traipsing halfway across the world because her highness is curious."

"What is it about this human that has you acting like this?" He waves a hand up and down. "You're in denial." He stops speaking suddenly, and in a blink, he's only inches in front of me. "You have feelings for her?" his voice is tainted with disgust.

"Don't be absurd," I say, sneering.

He bursts out laughing. "You never could lie, old friend. The casual nature between you two says otherwise, and the lack of your scent on her is telling. But no matter, the details are not important. Though whatever it is, hurry and be done with it soon. Fuck her and mark her or kill her if you must. Do whatever you need to get her out of your system—but do it before the winter solstice."

The sound of hoofbeats thundering up the road silences any further words on the tip of my tongue. For the second time today, a carriage comes into view over the hill, this one led by horses so black, even the moonlight doesn't shine on their coats.

"Elizabeth will expect you to give in to her now that you have claimed a human at last," Lawrence says quietly.

My stomach churns at the thought.

The carriage pulls up to the front, and from within, three figures clad in black step out.

Clara is out of time.

The others have arrived.

Continue the series in

THE VAMPIRE CURSE

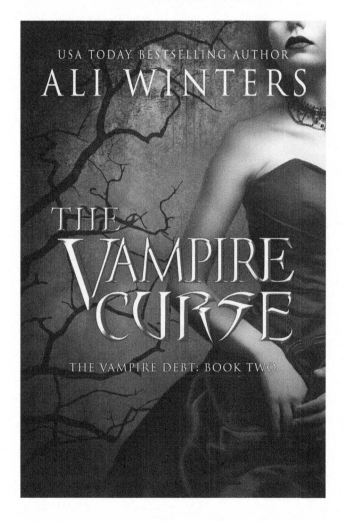

USA TODAY BESTSELLING AUTHOR
ALI WINTERS

THE VAMPIRE CURSE

THE VAMPIRE DEBT: BOOK TWO

ACKNOWLEDGEMENTS

And so ends the first book in another series. Clara and Alaric's story is only just beginning and they have a lot more to tell and I hope you stick around.

Acknowledgments are hard because there are countless people to thank for being part of my support system and my mind likes to go blank. So I will keep this short and sweet. I've had this story in my head for years now. This is truly a book(series) of my heart.

I never would have finished this book if it wasn't for a handful of wonderful people.

Thank you, Jesikah Sundin, for being a light and listening to me, and walking me through things. Thank you for being a ray of sun during a very strange and dark time in this world.

As always, thank you to Trish, Kitty, Kristine, April, and Jon. You all mean the world to me and I'm so glad I found such a wonderful group of weirdos.

Thank you, Alexis for everything you've done last minute and all of your ideas, and mostly, keeping me focused on what I needed to do.

Thank you to, Michelle, for all your hard work and helping me so I could focus on writing.

As always, thank you to my parents for always believing in me and nurturing my dreams through the good and bad times... especially the bad. And for your unwavering faith.

Thank you to all my friends I haven't named here, (the list would be impossibly long,) who've been there when I needed a shoulder. Who cheered me on, sprinted with me, and worked as a sounding board for ideas, and so much more.

To my husband for forcing me to keep a schedule of sleeping, eating, and working out so I could continue to function.

And last but never least, a million and one thank yous to my fans, thank you for continuing this journey with me! I couldn't be do what I love without you. Or if you're picking up my work for the first time, thank you for joining us!

ABOUT THE AUTHOR

Ali Winters is the USA TODAY Bestselling author of several series filled with romance, magic, and adventure.

Her first love will always be fantasy, but she fully admits to being obsessed with coffee and T-Rex, and has a weakness for love interests that walk the line between gray and villainy.

Ali was born and raised in the PNW but now currently resides in the wastelands that time forgot, with impossibly cold winters, and summers that are too short. She spends her days with her husband and alpha of her two dog pack. (They have assimilated her as one of their own and since she's the only one with opposable thumbs, have made her their leader.)

When she's not consumed with creating magical worlds for readers to get lost in, she can be found walking, reading, designing graphics, and creating art in various mediums.

Visit Ali on the web at www.aliwinters.com
Facebook.com/authoraliwinters
instagram.com/authoraliwinters

To learn more about The Vampire Debt
www.thevampiredebt.com
To subscribe to Ali's monthly newsletter for new releases,
exclusive sneak peeks, and visit
www.aliwinters.com/newsletter

Made in the USA
Monee, IL
15 August 2021

75720446R00166